Rosie's Troubles

ANN CARROLL

POOLBEG

For my Mother,
Mary O'Hara

Published in 1996 by
Poolbeg Press Ltd
123 Grange Hill, Baldoyle
Dublin 13, Ireland
E-mail: poolbeg@poolbeg.com

© Ann Carroll 1996

Copyright for typesetting, layout, design
© Poolbeg Press Ltd

The moral right of the author has been asserted.

3 5 7 9 10 8 6 4

A catalogue record for this book is available from the British Library.

ISBN 1 85371 681 2

Set by Poolbeg Group Services Ltd
Printed and bound by Nørhaven A/S
Viborg, Denmark

Characters

1995

Rosie McGrath.
Her gran.
Helena Gavin – Rosie's friend.
Mrs Gavin – Helena's mom.
Miss Graham, the sixth class teacher.

1920

Rosie.
Lilian Hennessey (Rosie's gran aged twelve).
Lilian's parents, Mr and Mrs Hennessey and her brothers Joseph, Christy and Jamesie.
Catherine Dalton, Lilian's friend who lives in the same tenement.
Tenement neighbours.
William Scott, a great friend of Catherine's. He works in the Gresham.
Hugh O'Callaghan, head porter at the Gresham.
Foley, a young IRA man. One of Michael Collins's "apostles," so called because they were twelve in number.
Clancy, another apostle.
Brown, a vicious Black and Tan soldier.
His partner who was a decent fellow (not named).
McLean, Smith, Cadlow, Wilde, and McCormack – all British agents.

Chapter 1

"RATS WERE the worst torment," Miss Graham informed her sixth class. "They were so daring they'd eat the dinner off your plate, that's if you had any dinner in the first place." The teacher paused and frowned.

Rosie McGrath was staring out the window, showing no interest at all.

Miss Graham was describing the lives of the poor in Dublin's 1920s. The silence became longer. Now the entire class was looking. Her friend Helena decided against a dig in the ribs. Last time she'd tried that, Rosie had shouted indignantly and walloped her, aggravating the teacher even more.

By now Miss Graham was breathing heavily. "What did I just say, Rosie McGrath? *Rosie McGrath!*"

Rosie jumped, wrenched back from Friday afternoon dreamland. The teacher expected an answer and her mind fumbled for Miss Graham's last words. Nothing.

"Yes Miss, of course, that's right," she tried optimistically. The class sniggered.

Miss Graham stared coldly at the twelve-year-old. Through clenched teeth she demanded, "What – exactly – did – I – say?"

Beside her, Helena whispered, "Rats."

Rosie trusted Helena with her life. "You were talking about rats, Miss."

The teacher wasn't fooled, "What about them?"

Helena muttered, "Poor people. 1920s. Dinner."

Her friend grappled, then beamed, "In the 1920s Miss, poor people had to eat rats for dinner."

When Helena groaned and the class tittered, Rosie knew she was way off the mark.

The teacher glared, "Next time you are inattentive, a four-page essay will follow. Now let's get back to this project on the Rare Ould Times."

"Just my luck," Rosie thought, "Shane and Hattie get a trip to Boston with Aunt Rose and Uncle Henry, and all I get is a boring project." She switched off again, staring out at the dull November afternoon, envying her cousins on their way to the States.

"It's not fair," had been her response when Mom had told her the news.

"Well it's hardly a pleasure trip, Rosie," Mom was exasperated, "Uncle Henry's sister is quite ill and it's natural her only relatives should pay a visit."

But to Rosie the trip was a big adventure from which she was excluded. "They'll miss school," she sighed. "Two whole weeks. No homework, no class work, no teachers, no rules, no orders, no nagging, no Miss Groucho Graham – " Rosie was getting carried away and would have gone on forever if she hadn't caught her mother's eye.

Hastily she changed tack. "Education is *so* important," she proclaimed piously, "and they'll be really far behind when they come back."

She thought of the tedious days ahead without her cousins and her bad humour deepened. "Anyway, I don't see how Hattie and Shane could be good for a sick person. If you ask my opinion, a sick person'd be much worse after a visit from those two, especially Shane. A sick person'd nearly – what's the matter?"

Mom's eyes were blazing and at last Rosie recognised the danger signals.

"You are extremely selfish," Madge said, "Just because you can't go, you wish they couldn't. Their aunt *asked* to see them, Rosie. She wants them."

"She must be very sick so!" Rosie muttered, then half -ashamed, "I was only thinking of school and how much work they'll miss."

"That's very nice of you," Mom was sweet, "so you won't mind copying out notes for them and making a list of what you've done every day they're away. I must say your concern does you credit!"

Rosie groaned. It *wasn't* fair. Not only were her cousins getting a trip she would've killed for, but Mom and Dad were off as well – to Brussels, for Dad's firm.

Could she not go with them? she'd asked, thoroughly dismayed.

"But Rosie, you'd hate to miss school!" Mom had said very smartly. Then, seeing her daughter's disappointment, went on more gently, "It's not possible, Rosie. We have to meet some of your father's colleagues on business and you'd be out of place. Anyway, Gran needs your company."

"Going away isn't always so marvellous!" Dad hastened to add. "Sometimes the best part is coming home."

How would I know? she thought sourly. I never get to go away.

So no trip to America, no trip to Brussels and her cousins' work to do as well as her own. She was one of life's deprived. A neglected child. "Maybe I could sue. That'd make them sorry!" She was sunk in gloom.

"Have you taken down *anything* I've put on the board?" Rosie half leaped out of her chair. Miss Graham was standing beside her, very angry.

"Sorry, Miss, I was thinking."

"Really. This is not something you do often, is it, Rosie?" Her voice became sugary. "Must be a terrible strain. Still, practice makes perfect, so you can put on your thinking cap and do a four-page essay over the weekend on 'My Most Interesting Thoughts'." The teacher flounced back to the blackboard.

Rosie's first most interesting thoughts were murderous. She wanted to kill Miss Graham. Sarcastic grump! She stuck out her tongue and screwed up her eyes at the retreating form and then froze when the teacher suddenly turned round.

"What *are* you doing?" Miss Graham stared at the child's gargoyle face.

"I think there's a pimple on my tongue, Miss." Rosie's eyes were crossed now in a pretence of examining the tip of her tongue.

"Would you like an essay about the offending pustule?" Miss Graham's voice was deceptively soft.

Rosie blinked. What *was* an offending pustule? She certainly didn't want another essay, "No thank you, Miss."

"Then keep you tongue in your mouth where it belongs. Perhaps you might even consider swallowing it – as a favour to me – because when you are not dreaming you are constantly talking. Now I suggest you write down what's on the board."

Rosie at last took her pen and concentrated.

Project:	The Rare Old Times
Method:	Interview with a grandparent or other old person about their childhood

Information sought on the following topics:

1. Living Conditions
2. School
3. Forms of entertainment
4. Friends
5. Customs and habits long ago

"Of course, we are far better off now," Miss Graham was saying, "we have more *things*, better health, etc. But there was hardly any crime then. That's why we call them the good old days. People were much nicer to each other. They treated each other with respect."

The bell rang for the end of the day.

"You!" she jabbed a finger in Rosie's direction, "Have that essay on this desk first thing on Monday morning. Otherwise you will be severely punished." She appeared suddenly struck by something – 'My Most Interesting Thoughts,' she ruminated, "Dear me! I do hope it's not four blank pages." And gathering up her books, the teacher sniggered at her own witticism.

"I hate Miss Graham," Rosie said to Helena once they were outside the school, "She's always so horrible." They were standing at the bus stop and Rosie was fed up.

"Maybe if you listened sometimes," Helena said mildly. But life's miseries piled on top of her friend.

"Everything is boring," she wailed. "Shane and Hattie are away and so are Mom and Dad. You don't live near. I've a revolting essay to do and I've no one to talk to for the weekend except Gran!"

Helena flagged down the approaching bus and, stepping on, smiled back at her friend.

"Do your project," she called, "get your gran to tell you all about the good old days!"

"*Moron!*" Rosie yelled. Inside the bus Helena laughed and waved goodbye.

How did anyone survive in those days? Rosie wondered. The fifties were bad enough. She remembered only too well her trip to 1956 and her shock when she found there were no TVs, no Walkmans, no McDonald's and no computer games. So the twenties must've been really primitive. How on earth had people passed their time? Maybe they slept a lot. Maybe they went into a coma for years from tedium.

Saturday brought rain and afternoon sport on television. Bor*ing!*

Gran and Rosie were in the sitting-room. The old lady was reading a book on Dublin tenement life. Her granddaughter fidgeted. There was nothing to do. She pulled her fingers, getting the joints to crack. She tried wiggling her ears. Then, rolling up her tongue, she attempted a piercing whistle. Failure.

"Why are you hissing?" Gran looked at her tortured expression. "Are you in pain?"

Rosie shook her head and the old lady continued reading.

Her granddaughter studied the front cover. Two women holding buckets and cloths stared back at her. The aprons over their long skirts were so white Rosie reckoned they hadn't yet started the day's cleaning. Still they looked worn out, one making an effort to smile, the other too weary to do more than stare. Behind them, in the background, were wet muddy streets, ramshackle buildings and the blurred figure of a girl beside a broken-down cart. What age was she, this girl? Fifteen, sixteen? What kind of life did she lead in those streets?

"Gran, what were you like when you were my age?"

Gran put down her book, "Surely you're tired of all that Rosie. You've heard my stories so many times before."

True, but she hadn't properly listened to them. To the twelve-year-old, Gran's childhood might as well have taken place on Mars. Looking back from the end of the twentieth century to near the beginning, the distance was huge. For Rosie, Gran's childhood was a blurred picture, like an old photograph in a history book. She could not recognise it as real life.

"What used you do all day, Gran? You can't have had much fun."

Gran smiled, "I had more fun than you're having now, waiting for the telly to come on, making conversation with me. Time passed very quickly, I can tell you." She was silent, then – "You know, Rosie, it's over seventy-five years since I was twelve. I bet you think that's a long, long time ago."

"Oh that's *ages! Centuries,*" Rosie agreed, never a diplomatic child.

"Not to me. You look at me and you see an old woman. I look in the mirror and, if I want, I can see myself at twelve years of age as if it were yesterday. Not only that, I can see my mother and father. And my brothers, Joseph, Jamesie and Christy, still trick-acting and wrestling. I can see the room we lived in, in North Great George's Street. The upstairs front on the first floor with the worn floorboards and poor miserable bits of furniture. I can even see the old sheets we hung for

7

screens around the beds, so we might all have a bit of privacy. None of this is far away to me, Rosie. I've carried it all with me, clear as day. Look."

She lifted a framed photograph from the mantelpiece, so familiar to her granddaughter it was part of the furniture – never properly examined.

"If I close my eyes, I'm back in that picture," she said. "In Mr Martin's photographic studio on Westmoreland Street. On the occasion of Joseph's confirmation."

Lovingly she fingered the image, as if she could feel the texture of the cloth and the soft skin of the faces.

Rosie saw a seated lady, hair parted in the middle and pinned up, wearing a high-necked blouse with little pleats down the front. Her skirt was so long the shoes were invisible. This was her great-grandmother. Standing on each side of her, their hands clutching hers, were two small boys, maybe seven and eight years old. They wore velvet knee-length trousers with little buttons down the side. Weird! Rosie thought. Their shoes are like girls' with those straps across the middle. Gross! Worse than the fifties!

Behind the boys stood Gran and Uncle Joseph, both dressed in sombre colours. Joseph's collar was so tight, Rosie wondered why his eyes weren't bulging. He was a little less tall than Gran. Between them, one hand resting on his wife's shoulder, was a tall bearded man. Very hairy, Rosie thought. I wonder how long it took to grow that beard down to his chest? It's like a woolly rug.

Her great-grandfather stared at her crossly.

"Nobody said 'Cheese'," Rosie mused.

"What?"

"None of them is smiling." She studied the solemn faces, "You'd think they'd just been told something awesome, like if they smiled the building would collapse on top of them."

"Don't be silly," Gran said, "Serious expressions were fashionable. That was a very happy day. As I said, it was Joseph's confirmation. We were wearing our best. Mother had foraged for months in the Daisy Market, putting those outfits together. I remember we felt *so* swanky! She'd saved for the photographer. In the end she hadn't enough and borrowed the rest from a moneylender. This is our only family photo."

Once more she studied the picture intently. "That chair had one bad leg," she said, "and nearly collapsed under Mother. Mr Martin had his head under the cloth, just about to take the photo, when the leg moved and Mother fell against Jamesie, who immediately sat down on the floor. Christy took a fit of the giggles. Father had to hold Mother upright and we were all laughing, except poor Mr Martin who said if we didn't behave ourselves he'd take the picture just as we were. I wish he had. Instead, he ordered Father to grip Mother by the shoulder and keep the chair stable. Under no circumstances were we to move until he'd finished. It's a miracle he got the boys to stay still. And Father was worse. He had to keep frowning so he wouldn't burst out laughing." She smiled, remembering. "How lively we were." Her voice became serious. "To think this is all I have left of them."

Rosie remembered her great-uncle Christy – Father Christy the priest, a white-haired man with a weak voice and a walking stick. Not someone given to uncontrollable fits of the giggles. And when she looked at Gran's kindly face she could see no trace of the girl in the photograph. Gran was very old.

"I am, amn't I?" The old lady read her thoughts and

smiled. "It's not surprising you should think so. After all, I was your age in 1920. But I remember it all so well."

For some minutes they were lost in thought. Then Gran broke the silence.

"Do you know what I remember best?" Her eyes were focused on another age and Rosie waited.

"I remember my friend Catherine Dalton. I don't even have to close my eyes to see her. Slim, dark-haired, full of fun, my best friend. She lived in the room over ours. November 1920 wasn't a good time for her."

She stopped and Rosie, her interest kindling, prompted, "Why not Gran?"

"A number of reasons. It was tough for us all living in the tenement. Even with my father and the boys having odd jobs, finding the money for food and fuel was hard. But Catherine's father went to England, looking for work, and they hadn't heard from him for ages. That November her mother was very sick. Everything went wrong for them. There was one particularly bad week I'll never forget, Rosie."

Her granddaughter stayed quiet, waiting for the old lady to continue at her own pace.

"Such troubled times. Mrs Dalton went into hospital on the Monday and Catherine was left on her own. She was the only child and her mother had always been a bit delicate. They had no relatives and she didn't want Catherine put into a home. 'Mr Dalton'd be so anxious, Mrs Hennessey,' she said to Mother, 'if he came home and didn't find us, he'd fret with worry.' So, of course, Mother promised to keep an eye on Catherine." Gran smiled, "She wasn't too easy to keep an eye on. Together we used to get up to terrible mischief. 'Here come Trouble and Torment', the neighbours always said."

Rosie's mouth dropped. Trouble and Torment didn't seem at all suitable names for Gran. Fragile and Frail, maybe.

"In 1916, during Easter week when we were only eight, we sneaked down to O'Connell Street – Sackville Street it was then. It was the noise that attracted us. Not gunfire. The noise of looters, of breaking glass and shouting. People running into shops empty-handed and coming out with clothes or food or furniture. There was practically a procession staggering along with tables and sofas." She giggled, "We saw one fella wheeling his girlfriend up Talbot Street in an armchair with castors. Mothers were running along with prams. No babies in them, just groceries or bales of material. I saw a huge rocking-horse in one pram. We thought this was great fun and dashed into Findlater's. Next minute the police arrived. Well, I didn't want to leave empty-handed. Father liked a drink and Findlater's stocked lots of wines. Only I couldn't read too well, so I grabbed a likely bottle and hid it under my pinafore. Catherine was already on her way to the window – empty-handed, but walking very oddly. I flew past her. 'The polis is coming. Hurry up,' I yelled. She was waddling like a penguin and I had to help her place her feet over the broken glass. Her legs felt enormous. She lumbered down the street after me and once around the corner took four huge bags of sugar out of her drawers. She gave me two. Mother clipped my ears for looting and thanked me for the sugar. Father said a bottle of vinegar was *not* the same as a bottle of wine and the sooner I learned to read the better."

Picturing the eight-year-old Catherine Dalton struggling out of the shop, Rosie thought she sounded great fun.

11

"Oh she was," Gran agreed, "and brave too. Once, when we were your age, we were playing on the front steps and a young fella dashed past us into the hall and down the stairs. The back door was jammed and he couldn't get it opened. Next minute a lorry load of Black-and-Tans screeched to a halt in front of us.

'Did you see anything suspicious?' They were roaring at us and pointing guns and I couldn't say a word with terror.

'No, sir,' Catherine said. 'We saw nothing. Except one young fella who ran up the road and around the corner. Isn't that right, Lilian?' She was so cool. I nodded – and kept nodding with fright and Catherine said, very calmly, 'Your head will fall off if you don't stop doing that, Lilian.' She went back to skipping and, after a minute or two, the lorry went on. They didn't know what to make of her. The young fella was very grateful though."

"The Black-and-Tans, were they the British Army?" Rosie struggled to recall her history.

"They were an extra police force," Gran said, "brought from England. Everyone thought they were convicts, offered their freedom if they joined up and served over here. Some of them were vicious. They didn't have a proper uniform, with their dark berets and khaki jackets. That's where they got their name. They raided homes for no reason and smashed up everything. 'This stuff is useless anyway,' they'd say, 'We're doing you a favour Missus!' If you objected they'd arrest you. Many a young innocent man was found dead in an alleyway after being arrested by the Tans." Gran's eyes were fierce with indignation. Then all of a sudden she looked drained, tired out.

Rosie wanted to get back to Catherine Dalton.

"What happened to your friend, Gran? Why do you remember that week so well?"

"I'll tell you tomorrow, Rosie. All this talk is making me a little weary."

During the evening Rosie found herself thinking of the past, of the tenement house and the photograph, of young Lilian Hennessey and her lively brothers. But most of all she was drawn to Catherine Dalton. Brave, adventurous, great fun. If Rosie had been alive three-quarters of a century ago, she knew they could have been great friends. She found herself looking forward to hearing all about the girl.

It occurred to her that Gran's childhood wasn't so boring after all.

Chapter 2

ON SUNDAY afternoon, while the blazing fire kept the grey November weather at bay, Gran continued her story as if she'd never left off.

"There's no other week in my memory quite like that one," she said, settling into her armchair opposite Rosie. "First, Catherine was on her own. She wanted to keep a sense of home for when her mother came out of hospital. And she never gave up on her father. If he returned, she didn't want him to find their room deserted. Even though we tried to insist, she wouldn't move in with us."

"But your family must have been like sardines in a tin," Rosie said. "You had no space for anyone else!"

"If we could fit six in a room we could fit seven," Gran said, defying Rosie's sense of logic. "Anyway, space had nothing to do with it. A young girl was very vulnerable on her own if the Tans raided. The Troubles were so bad, no one in our area went to school that week!"

Rosie was amazed. In her book, days off school were *definitely* not classed as troubles. People must have had funny brains in those days. Maybe their minds were affected from squashing big numbers into small spaces. Not enough oxygen getting to the head.

14

"It must've been smashing having no school," she said wistfully. "I wouldn't have thought that'd be a trouble to anybody – except maybe teachers. Everyone knows they love school but that's only 'cos they like torturing kids."

Gran looked at her pityingly. "There was shooting in the streets, Rosie, you could get caught in the crossfire. People were killed and you never knew when there'd be a raid. There was a 10 pm curfew and at midnight all the street lights went out. Everywhere was pitch black. They were frightening, dangerous times, with ambushes and murders."

Rosie was taken aback. Those weren't troubles. Troubles were the minor irritations of life, like not enough pocket money or not being allowed to use the dishwasher or watch telly – and of course school. Maybe school wasn't so minor, but at least it wasn't murder and mayhem.

"Why did you call those days the Troubles? Wasn't the name a bit . . . a bit . . ."

"Feeble?" Gran finished, I don't know why we used that. There were some dreadful atrocities." Her eyes were sad and she took some moments before resuming her story.

"Anyway," she continued, "Catherine wasn't on her own for long. She took in a stranger, a homeless girl she met on the street." Gran frowned, her disapproval fresh after all these years.

"Was that not a kind thing to do?" Rosie asked, warming more and more towards Catherine.

"It was, I suppose. But there was something creepy about that girl. She was only there for the week and I cannot recall her name, yet the first time I saw her I had the strangest feeling we knew each other, although I

15

was certain we'd never met . . . such a strong sense of familiarity." She shook her head, puzzled still.

"Did you not like her?" Rosie asked.

"I was afraid of her. I didn't see her that much because I had the flu and wasn't allowed out. But a couple of times she spoke about the future as if she knew exactly what unhappiness it contained. She made me shiver . . ." Gran trailed off and what had been a steady flicker of interest in Rosie now became a flame.

"Why? What did she say, Gran?"

"Well . . . she knew something was going to happen the next weekend, on the Sunday . . ." Again she broke off, her eyes half closing as the memories flooded back.

"Sunday the 21st of November 1920," she mused. "Who could ever forget it? Anyway, this girl warned Catherine not to go to Croke Park for the match. Catherine thought she was daft. Everyone was going to it. Father was taking the boys. Catherine had been looking forward to it for ages. So was I and we were going with William Scott. He was a great pal of Catherine's. A very kind boy. He was a Boots in the Gresham Hotel, which meant he had to polish all the guests' footwear. It was a live-in position. William was an orphan, his only relative an uncle in Inchicore who spent most of his time at sea. Catherine became his best friend and, whenever he could, he helped her out with leftover food from the kitchen.

"William was mad keen on football and weeks beforehand he arranged to have that Sunday afternoon off. He couldn't wait to see Dublin beat Tipperary in the challenge match. Then along came this stranger, trying to ruin everything with her talk of violence and death. Only Catherine wouldn't let her.

"In the event, I wasn't better so I couldn't go, and in

spite of all her frightening talk it was the stranger who went with them.

"Her warnings were right. The day was full of killing. Some British agents had been shot in the morning. In revenge, the Tans turned up at Croke Park and fired on the crowd. Father got your uncles got out, unharmed. And he saw William at one of the exits, but not the girls. I never saw Catherine again. She never came home."

What on earth did Gran mean? Was Catherine killed? Her anxiety sharp, Rosie had to know and did not stop to wonder why she should care what had happened to someone over seventy-five years ago.

"Why didn't she come home? *Please*, Gran."

"I don't know. There was some shooting on the streets and Mother wouldn't let me out that night to look for her. I waited up hours. And when there was no sign I thought she must've been shot.

"Next day I read the papers but she wasn't in any reports of dead or wounded. They didn't have all the names, but no girl her age had been killed or injured. When mother went to the shops in the afternoon, I called in to the Gresham to see if William knew where she was. The place was in an uproar because Mr Callaghan the hall porter had been lifted that morning and brought in for questioning by the Tans. Anyway, after a lot of waiting I was told William had gone straight out to Inchicore after the match. His uncle's ship was in and William was to stay with him for a week.

"Then I set off for Jervis Street, where Mrs Dalton was, to see if *she'd* any news. Only Mrs Dalton had left the hospital on the Sunday, sometime in the evening. The staff were so busy after the match, no one had

17

noticed her leaving. She never came home either. Both of them, mother and daughter, vanished."

Rosie was incredulous. People did not disappear into thin air. Why didn't Gran go to the police?

"The police!" the old lady snorted, "The police were not our friends. We didn't take our worries to them."

"But someone must have seen her. What about the girl? The stranger?"

"The last I heard of the stranger was on the Monday, from a neighbour, Mr Dempsey who'd been at Croke Park. He'd seen the girl standing there, while the crowd swarmed around her. Then he got pushed and carried along and lost sight of her.

"He remembered the girl though, because she was so calm in the face of all that madness. The Tans were firing on the crowd and there was a stampede for the exits.

"'In all that panic,' he said, 'no one pushed her. A space was left around her. Others were trampled on as people clambered and clawed their way out. She was the only person not moving among those thousands!'"

Rosie closed her eyes and visualised the scene. At the four corners of the field she saw the lorries. Armed men streamed across the pitch, firing. She heard the screams, the gasping breath of fear, the trampling feet. Terror hung in the air like a foul smell.

Through the noise she heard someone call, "Rosie, hurry up! You'll be killed! Don't stay there. Hurry up! Rosie!" The voice was urgent, young. Then all the clamour faded.

"So you never saw that girl again?"

"I didn't. But the neighbour who'd been at the match did. About nine o'clock that Sunday night he heard a noise on the pavement below. The streets were deserted. Only a lunatic would have ventured out. Mr Dempsey peered from the window and saw a shadowy form. Then from somewhere a light came and the girl was centred in the beam. She was carrying an army kit bag. She must have seen the neighbour because she waved. Then the light went and she was gone."

Rosie frowned. Was this some kind of hoax? Some trick Gran was playing for her own amusement? "Another disappearing act? Come on, Gran!"

"I don't know," the old lady shrugged, "I don't much care either. I told you, I'd been sick for a fortnight, so I wasn't able to see much of Catherine. I didn't really get to know that girl. I didn't want to. For Catherine's sake, I was friendly enough with her at the end. But she brought bad luck with all her fearful talk."

"She could have waited a few more days to see if Catherine came back."

Gran sighed, "That's what I thought. But what if she knew Catherine wasn't coming back? What if she looked into the future and saw there was no hope?"

"Why didn't you search for her? Ask her?"

"There was no point. Dublin was full of homeless people and I knew little about her. Anyway, the ones I cared about were Catherine and her mother, and of them there was no trace. Only an empty room, untouched, intact. It was as if they'd gone from the face of the earth."

Refusing to accept what she said, Rosie fought against Gran's resignation.

"People don't vanish, Gran. There has to be an explanation."

"What explanation, Rosie? I've thought about it often. Loss of memory? It could happen to one of them, not both. Murder? No bodies were found. Who would have deliberately killed them? Not even the Tans. And if they had, they wouldn't have bothered to hide the corpses. They could get away with murder.

"If they weren't killed, did they run away from some awful trouble? Perhaps. But then Catherine would have written to me.

"So many poor people at the time couldn't read or write, but she was that proud of her skills, she used to put notes under the door sometimes, when she could have knocked instead. She wasn't the type, Rosie, to leave a friend without any farewells."

Gran crossed the room to the bureau. From a drawer she took an old tin, then rifling through some papers, she selected three and gave them to her granddaughter.

"These will show the kind of person she was."

Rosie fingered the letters. They were written on thick yellowish squares, uneven at the edges.

"Butchers' wrapping paper," Gran said, "she'd no money for proper writing sheets."

The words were carefully formed, the writing large, in thick pencil, faded with the years. She began to read.

Second Upstairs Front
Wednesday 3rd November
8 o'clock

To Lilian,

Having no money is terrible! Mother sent me to O'Shea's pawnshop after school. I was to bring Father's silver-framed photograph — the one good thing we own — and get eight shillings. It was shocking to think of him, all happy and smiling in his good suit, sitting in that horrible place for a week. He

20

could be next to Mr Dempsey's smelly shoes. Father hates Mr Dempsey. Worse, he could have Mrs Reilly's African Mission snake wrapped around him. Our family is not fond of snakes.

I had a wonderful idea and wrapped up a piece of wood instead, using lots of newspaper and a hundred knots. Sometimes, if he knows you, Mr O'Shea won't open the parcel. Only this time he did. I nearly fainted when he asked everyone in the shop was the wood a true likeness of father. But he got a good laugh and gave me four shillings with the pawn ticket.

Signed, Your Friend
Catherine Dalton.
PS Get better soon.

Rosie tried to picture a world where a twelve-year-old had to survive on her wits. Imagine having no money for food. Did anyone live like that now?

She thought how Mom always used a cheque or an Access card in the supermarket and never knew how much a full trolley would cost till she got to the checkout.

Miss Graham was wrong about the good old days. In Rosie's opinion they were horrible and she wondered how Catherine remained so cheerful? She turned to the next page.

Second Upstairs Front
Tuesday 9th November
9 o'clock

To Lilian,
You are so lucky not to be in Miss Gummer's class. She gave me all her darning to do in school. This is not fair,

but she says I have missed so much class there is no point trying to catch up. Is it my fault Mother isn't well?

Then Miss Gummer says the devil makes work for idle hands and that's why she gives me her sewing. Does she think I should thank her? Well I am not grateful and she is not a nice person.

Today I brought in Mrs O'Reilly's snake, which I sneaked out of her room. I sewed it down the inside of one of Miss Gummer's petticoats with the head sticking over the waist. It has a horrible look on its face, with its fangs bared. When she takes it out of the bag I hope she screams.

Signed, Your friend

Catherine Dalton.

PS Your mother says you will be well enough for me to visit next week.

Rosie was lost in admiration. Miss Gummer would have known instantly who tried to frighten her to death. Catherine would have been severely punished, maybe even beaten. Eagerly she turned to the next letter to see what happened.

Second Upstairs Front
Thursday 11th November
8 o'clock

To Lilian,

Best wishes in your sickness.

Miss Gummer said nothing. She must not have checked her sewing bag yet. I am so glad. Mrs Reilly thinks the Tans stole her snake. She says the last time they raided, one fellow had his eye on it and must have sneaked back. She is in mourning and would complain, but does not wish to be shot.

It was exciting today. The Tan lorries came speeding

22

along just when we got out of school and they were firing everywhere. No one was hit but a few windows were broken. Miss Gummer says if this continues the school will have to close. That will save me some darning.

Mother was sad when I got home, and she talked about Father. She was too sick today to go out and look for cleaning work. So we had no money for food again.

I went to see if William could help. On the way there was a shop in Great Britain Street with chickens hanging up outside. I kept seeing a plate with delicious cooked meat on it. The smell was beautiful. This made me very hungry and I could not help myself. I robbed one and ran.

Then I got a terrible fright when I saw a policeman. I walked along trying to look like a normal person, holding the chicken by the neck.

"Are you taking your pet for a walk?" he says, very sarcastic.

"No," I says, "Are you blind? This is no pet. This is a dead chicken I am taking home for my dinner."

He did not know what to say and while he was gaping I ran off. Mother was so glad she said nothing.

Signed, Your Friend
Catherine.

Once again Rosie was amazed at the lengths Catherine was forced to go to, just for bare survival. Yet she did not moan. Instead, life was a big adventure to her. She must have been so brave and daring. What a pity it was Rosie could not meet her.

Then, unbidden, came the thought, "Maybe I *could* meet her. Maybe I could go back to the past again. Perhaps I could even find out what happened to her!"

The idea gripped her imagination and for the rest of the afternoon she thought of nothing else.

Chapter 3

THE OPPORTUNITY arose unexpectedly. On Sunday evening Helena rang. "Mom says you can stay with us for the week if your gran doesn't mind. You can come home with me after school tomorrow. What do you think?"

"Brilliant!" Rosie said. Instantly she had a brain wave, but it needed working out. No point mentioning it yet. Putting Gran on the phone to Helena's mom, she prayed the old lady wouldn't object. After all, Rosie was supposed to keep her company.

"What a wonderful idea!" Gran said, "Now that I don't have to baby-sit I can play bridge every night with my friends."

Bridge! Rosie was miffed. Imagine preferring such a dull game to her marvellous company! She was not a small child who needed baby-sitting! How ungrateful! Gran did not deserve the efforts Rosie was going to make to find her friend. "But how will I find her?" she wondered. "How will I get back?"

She remembered her trip to the fifties. It had started when she'd been knocked unconscious by a car. Well, she had no intention of getting run over this time. So how was she to do it? She wished there was someone to

24

ask. Uncle Jack was the only person who knew she'd made a journey to the past. Maybe he could advise her. Almost instantly Rosie rejected the idea. He would not approve of a visit to such turbulent times.

She brooded, recalling his words after her last adventure, his explanation for what had happened. "Perhaps it was some kind of willpower on your part, Rosie. Single-minded determination has won a lot of battles for people. Maybe you have that kind of determination. And maybe that sudden blow to your head cleared some kind of route to the past."

She certainly had that kind of determination now. Perhaps the route was still open. Last time she had concentrated on Aunt Rose in surroundings familiar to her aunt's childhood. This time she would do the same with Catherine. But would it work?

There was only one way to find out.

Early next morning before Gran was up, Rosie packed her green rucksack. Food was going to be short in 1920. Seeing no reason to starve, she took a two-litre bottle of Coke, a loaf of bread from the freezer, a tub of butter, a pack of rashers, two tins of beans, four large bars of chocolate, peanut butter, some pot noodles, a box of muesli and a jar of jam. Mom had done the shopping before she left, which meant Gran wouldn't realise what was missing. For good measure she threw in a box of tea bags, her Polaroid camera, socks and her Nike air runners.

The bag was very heavy. Leaving it beside the hall door, she ran upstairs to say goodbye.

Startled out of her sleep, Gran was dazed. "Is it time for school already? I must have overslept." It was only seven-fifteen but Rosie did not enlighten her.

25

"No need to get up, Gran. I can see myself out. You go back to sleep."

"I will, if you don't mind. Poor Catherine Dalton was on my mind for hours last night. And William. Have a nice time, Rosie. Don't forget to ring and let me know how you're getting on."

"I'll call you sometime on Wednesday," Rosie promised. "Bye, Gran!"

It was half an hour by bus to her friend's house. Helena was taken aback to see Rosie.

"I thought you were coming after school." Then she grinned. "Your feet look funny," she said. Rosie was wearing the eighteen-hole Docs Dad had given her the year before. They were her pride and joy, although they were a bit tight now and did not go with her plaid uniform. Her lucky boots, she would not leave them behind. She had asked Mom for a new pair. "Definitely not!" the answer was sharp. "They make you look like a convict. I don't know what possessed your father. A nice pair of slip-ons would suit you better. You're bad enough with that spiky hair." Sometimes, Rosie thought, Mom's brain needed adjusting. If she had her way Rosie would be wearing neat dresses and have long hair with a bow in it.

Helena was shaking her head, "Miss Graham will throw a fit." She put on the teacher's prissy voice, "Rosie McGrath! Those hideous boots do not match your kilt. They are a disgrace to the good name of the school and fit only for hooligans and vandals. Write a four-page essay on 'Correct Uniform'. And please get a wig to cover that terrible hairstyle!"

Rosie sighed. In hospital, after her road accident, they'd shaved off her long fair hair to operate on her

26

head. She'd kept it spiky ever since. Too bad if Miss Graham didn't like it. But that wasn't what she wanted to talk about now.

"I'm not going to school," she said, "I'm not staying with you. I want you to do me a favour." Quickly, before Helena could interrupt and before anyone else came to the door, she went on, "I need you to cover for me, to give this to Miss Graham."

Helena took the note and read:

"Dear Miss Graham,
    For family reasons Rosie will be absent from school this week. I regret any inconvenience.
    Yours,
    Madge McGrath."

Helena's mouth dropped, "But your mom is away. This is a forgery."

"No it's not!" Rosie was indignant. "It's an old note. Miss Graham never kept it. I cut along the top where the date was. I hope she doesn't remember it. Will you give it to her?"

Helena nodded, then quickly hid the note, half shutting the door as her mother came into the hall.

"Rosie! I thought you weren't arriving till after school. Never mind, you're very welcome – though anybody would think Helena was trying to lock you out!"

Startled, Helena opened the door wide and Rosie almost fell in. She took a deep breath, "I had to come this morning, Mrs Gavin, to tell you I won't be staying. Gran needs me."

Mrs Gavin was staring at Rosie's boots and it took her a few moments to answer. "Extraordinary!" she murmured, dragging her eyes away. "I thought your gran was delighted. She wanted to play bridge."

"She just said that. She doesn't really play bridge."

Mrs Gavin's eyebrows rose. "But I've met her at tournaments."

Rosie groaned inwardly, "I mean she doesn't play any more – much." Mrs Gavin's eyebrows went higher and Rosie continued desperately, "It's her hearing. She's stone deaf. It gets her into trouble. Last time someone said 'two no trumps', Gran thought she and her partner were being called 'two old frumps.' She got really annoyed and told the woman she was a stupid cow. After that she was banned from the bridge club for rowdy behaviour."

Mrs Gavin's eyebrows had disappeared with disbelief. "But when I spoke to her on the telephone her hearing was fine!"

Oh God! Rosie swallowed and bluffed on. "Yes, well, she *is* fine on the telephone. She can hear perfect on the telephone. It's something to do with the electronics . . ." Rosie trailed off. She reckoned Mrs Gavin's eyebrows were now somewhere on the back of her head. The poor woman was totally bewildered.

"I just can't stay," Rosie said at last.

Helena's mom stared at her. She held her gaze. Then the eyebrows came back to base and Mrs Gavin smiled. "I understand. You don't want to leave an old lady on her own. You're a kind, thoughtful child."

Rosie squirmed and was relieved when Helena said they'd better be on their way.

"I hope you know what you're doing," Helena said. "Whatever you're up to, don't tell any more lies. You're very bad at it."

But Rosie was not listening. "I want you to do me

one more favour," she said. She'd almost forgotten. A simple slip-up could mean disaster. She had to make sure Gran didn't ring Mrs Gavin to ask after her. Helena would get into trouble and Gran would be so worried she might even drag Mom and Dad back from Brussels. Rosie shivered.

"On Wednesday," she said, "Gran always goes out to the community centre. Mrs Stacey, the home help, comes at ten-thirty. I want you to ring my house at small break. Ask Mrs Stacey to tell Gran that Rosie says everything is fine. OK?"

"But won't your gran want to talk to you during the week?"

"Not if she's playing bridge. A message will keep her happy. People who play bridge forget everything and don't want to think about anything else."

"What are you up to, Rosie?"

"I can't tell you. Not yet anyway. You'd think I was mad."

Helena's anxiety deepened. "Whatever it is, it doesn't sound like a good idea!"

"Oh it is! It is!" Rosie was fervent.

"But what if anything goes wrong? No one will have a clue where you are and everyone will blame me."

"Nothing will go wrong. Don't worry, I have it all worked out. I know what I'm doing."

Helena, who had seen her friend come through so many scrapes over the years, was more convinced by these words than Rosie.

They parted at the bus stop with Rosie taking the number 11 into town.

She stood outside the house in North Great George's Street, a somewhat odd figure in her anorak, green kilt and huge Doc Martens. These houses are beautiful, she thought, staring at the renovated exteriors. They mightn't let me in, looking like this.

For a moment she regretted the Docs. But they were her lucky boots, a prized gift. She couldn't have gone without them.

Up the road a middle-aged man was lifting a bicycle down some steps. He was wearing a suit but no overcoat. Rosie thought he looked too distinguished for a bicycle. He was a bit like a professor with his high balding forehead and his neat beard. Maybe it's all posh people who live here now, she worried. Then the man on the bicycle beamed at her as he passed and at once she felt better.

Looking up at the house, Rosie was aware of a figure at the second-storey window. Shielding her eyes against the wintry sun she focused. A girl was looking down at her, hand raised in greeting. Then the sunlight sparkled briefly on the glass and the figure vanished.

"Are you looking for something, young lady?" A man was on the doorstep picking up the milk bottles.

"Who's the girl at the window?" Rosie said. He glanced up then shook his head, "There isn't any girl, only myself and my wife and she's in the kitchen. You must be seeing things."

"I am not – there definitely was a girl. She has long dark hair. It's rude to tell someone they're seeing things!"

"Well, I'm telling you there is no girl. I ought to know who lives in my house. I certainly don't need a peculiar-looking kid to tell me!"

"I am not peculiar-looking!" Rosie was raging, "You should look in the mirror. You're too old for a nose ring and a ponytail." Oh, no. Instantly she regretted her words. He'd never let her in to the house now. He looked hurt.

"The young always think no one else should have any fun," he muttered.

"I'm sorry," Rosie felt bad. "I didn't mean to offend you. Actually I like nose rings."

He brightened at once. "And *I* like Docs," he said, "in fact I own a bright red pair."

"Deadly!" Rosie was sincere, "that's my favourite colour after purple."

The man looked as though he might pursue the subject, then changed his mind. "What are you doing here anyway – shouldn't you be at school?"

"I'm doing a school project," Rosie told him. "It's about my gran. She used to live in this house in 1920, in the front room on the first floor."

"Really! Well, you'd best come in then. By the way, I'm Harry Jones."

Rosie hesitated. All her life she'd been told not to talk to strange men, never mind follow them into their house. Mom, who judged by appearances, would definitely think this man was very strange.

An irate female in a dressing-gown appeared. "For God's sake, Harry, hurry up with the milk. Anyone would think you went out to find a cow! I'd like my cornflakes today, if it's not too much to ask!"

She stared at Rosie and the man explained her presence. At once Mrs Jones forgot her annoyance and smiled. "Why don't you bring her in then? I'll show her around. And you, Harry, should be on your way to work. You're dead late as it is."

Glancing at his watch Harry groaned, rushed inside and emerged a second later in an overcoat, carrying a briefcase. He kissed the air near his wife's cheek, wished Rosie good luck and was off.

Rosie followed Mrs Jones into the house.

"Now, I'll show you where your gran lived. I dare say it's changed since her day. Do you know, we even had to replace the floorboards. People just ripped them up and threw them on the fire. Can you believe the vandalism?" Rosie said nothing. Looking at her face, the woman shut up and led her to the first floor.

"In here?" Rosie stared at the four-poster bed, the high ceiling, intricate plasterwork and the beautiful Georgian fireplace, all lovingly restored. So this had been Gran's home.

"Sometimes I get carried away," the woman's voice was apologetic. "I forget how poor people were in those days. They must have been very cold and badly off to tear up the floorboards." Rosie nodded, wishing she would go. Mrs Jones read her thoughts. "I'll leave you on your own for a while. Have a good look round."

But this was not where Rosie's immediate interest lay. As soon as the woman had gone downstairs she tiptoed on to the landing. At first she heard only the distant murmur of the radio from the kitchen. She closed her eyes, "Where are you, Catherine?" she whispered over and over, like a kind of mantra.

The radio voices faded. Silence. Not a creak, not a rustle.

"Please. You must help."

Around her the stillness was so powerful she felt as if time had stopped and the house itself was waiting, suspending its breath until time creaked into motion again. New sounds wafted from the stairs. She strained to hear. The voices of women drew closer and more distinct. Finally they were beside her on the landing.

"Lady Caroline, what a charming portrait. And executed by Mr Reynolds if I'm not mistaken."

"Yes. And our new purchase, a Gainsborough landscape, is in the drawing-room. There is no one like Mr Gainsborough for evoking the pastoral scene, don't you think?"

Rosie shivered. She must not return to a different century. Panic gripped her. What if she made a mistake? If her trip took her farther back than Gran's childhood, she would be lost. She would know no one.

She tried to think. "What should I do, Catherine? Please."

She opened her eyes and could see no one but beneath the surface of her mind she could still hear those voices from the eighteenth century – the murmured conversation of Lady Caroline and her friend.

"Catherine – *please!*" In a panic she reached out to grip the banisters and a shaft of sunlight from the landing window sparkled on her watch. The voices disappeared. Rosie relaxed and glanced at the time. Nine o'clock. For some reason the date was blinking on and off. She took a sharp breath. Swiftly she adjusted the numbers. The watch stopped blinking.

15.11.1920 stared back at her.

Once again she closed her eyes and this time she concentrated on the date. It was a Monday morning, the day Catherine's mother went into hospital . . .

"Mrs Dalton, let me help you."

"The ambulance is here. Catherine, take your mother's arm."

"Please God the tests will be all right, Mrs Dalton, and all you need is a bit of a rest."

"Don't forget, Catherine. Keep the room nice in case your father comes home."

"I will, Mother. Don't worry."

"That room is our home. Your father will expect to find us there. It's where we belong."

Rosie heard footsteps and the sound of creaking stairs. She had a sense of people passing just beneath her, but when she looked she could see no one. The voices faded into silence.

Should she follow? "But they've all vanished," she thought. "I need a stronger connection to take me back."

She heard Mrs Dalton's words again. "That room is our home . . . it's where we belong."

Cautiously she made her way up to the second floor and stepped into Catherine's room. It was beautiful, the floor highly polished to show off the rich rugs and the antique furniture. Sunlight filtered through the tall window and drew her like a magnet. She could imagine Catherine standing here, watching out for her father.

The house began to move to a different rhythm. Voices upstairs and down, feet clattering, noises from other rooms. Breathing deeply Rosie became aware of a choking smell, stale and foul. "Not yet," she said, "not yet." She had a fearful dizzying sense of sliding in and out of time. Looking down she was half-reassured, half-disappointed by the usual morning traffic. Then, glancing at the shutter she caught her breath. Beneath the fresh paint, she could make out a name etched into the wood with some sharp instrument. *Catherine*. Her head swam. She was about to travel back more than seventy-five years. Such a distance. Such a foreign place.

Afraid, she played for time, tracing the letters on the shutter. If she didn't go back, no one would ever know what happened to Catherine Dalton.

"Don't be afraid, Rosie," a young voice murmured.

"I need more time," she said.

Now her head was full of whispering, words from the past and the present:

"Time is what this journey is all about."

"Such a terrible week."

"You've found a route to the past."

"Such dreadful times."

"Willpower and determination! That's all you need."

"Whatever you're planning, it doesn't sound like a good idea."

"Don't be afraid, Rosie."

She knew the last voice was Catherine's. "Where are you?"

"I'm waiting, down on the street."

Refusing to think further, Rosie rushed from the room, down the two flights of stairs to the hall. In a panic, she pulled at the heavy front door as if she would never escape. Mrs Jones came out into the passage and called to her, but she did not hear.

Outside she leaned against the railings, breathless, eyes closed. I am so scared, she thought, it's so dangerous. But I want to go back. I must.

She tried to relax then, concentrating on another age. She heard the shift in time, the change from cars and blaring horns to clopping hooves and trundling cartwheels.

Someone was tugging at her sleeve, "Are you all right? You look as if you might faint. Are you dizzy?"

Rosie opened her eyes.

Chapter 4

BESIDE HER stood the girl she had seen at the window.
Rosie recognised her face, the striking contrast
between her pale features and long dark hair. Now the
girl was gripping her arm. "Don't fall. Lean against the
railings." Rosie did as she was told, her head reeling
from the shock of the new – or the very old. When her
brain cleared, she took a deep breath.

"That's better," the girl said, "you're getting your
strength back."

The street was totally changed. Cobblestones glinted
in the frosty sunlight. Instead of cars and lorries there
were a few horses and carts. The houses were
dilapidated, the glass gone in fanlights, the paint
cracked and peeling. In some cases the front doors were
missing. Tattered curtains hung in the windows and
above them, all along the street, were lines of washing
stretched out on poles.

But what Rosie noticed most, what really assaulted
her senses and made her feel sick was the *smell*. It took
her some moments to realise this was coming from the
heaps of horse manure on the road. Some of it was
steaming. "Oh, that is *so* disgusting!" she said and held
her nose.

Her companion was puzzled, "What are you talking about?"

"Those horses. Using the road as a toilet!"

"What do you expect them to use?" She giggled. "Not the public toilets? Imagine them going down into the gents in Sackville Street! What a fright the gents would get!"

Rosie laughed at the image and the girl smiled. "That's better." Men were moving along the road now, shovelling the stuff on to carts. "I wonder what they do with it," she said.

The girl shrugged. "They probably bring it to the parks, put it on the flower-beds." Bored with the subject, she looked at Rosie with interest. "What's your name?"

"Rosie McGrath."

"Uhuh. And how did you get here? Where do you live?"

Rosie rubbed her forehead. "I'm not sure how I got here and I don't know if I have a home right now."

The girl nodded sagely. "You've lost your memory. That's why you felt so dizzy and weak. You're a mystery person!" She was gleeful. "I love a mystery. I don't know how you got here either. One minute I was leaving Mother on to the ambulance and there was no one around except Mrs Reilly. Next minute there you were, all pale and dizzy. At least you know your name. Do you think you got a blow on the head?"

"Not this time," Rosie muttered, but the girl wasn't listening. Instead she was frowning with concentration. Then she said triumphantly, "I know what it is you've got. You've got ammonia!"

Rosie thought hard. "Amnesia," she said.

"Exactly. You can stay with me if you like, till you

remember everything." She hesitated, then said, "It'd be nice if you did. Mother's gone into Jervis Street. I can't visit her till Wednesday night. I'll be on my own if you don't stay."

"You must be Catherine Dalton, so!" Rosie spoke without thinking.

"How do you know?"

"You were talking to someone." She was vague.

"Mrs Reilly," Catherine nodded. "She helped me bring Mother down to the ambulance. But like I said, I could have sworn there was no one else here."

Her eyes narrowed and she looked intently at Rosie, who shifted awkwardly, trying to think of a plausible explanation for her sudden appearance. But Catherine supplied her own answer. "You must have come when I was helping Mother into the ambulance, even though it only took a minute. There's no other possible explanation."

"I'd love to stay with you." Rosie was anxious to change the subject.

"Smashing," Catherine said and they took stock of each other. The girl was very thin, Rosie thought. Her dark eyes were huge in the small pale face. Her dress was long and neat but patched, faded to a dull blue.

"Why, you've no shoes!" Rosie blurted. The girl went a bright red and her feet squirmed, trying to hide. "I will have when Father comes home," she said, "he'll buy me button boots and a satin dress for Christmas." She looked sad, but Rosie had just noticed her own clothes and was too astonished to pay attention.

She knew from her trip to the fifties that her appearance would change with the change of time and she would be left with only a few items from the present. But she had not expected to look *so* hideous.

Oh, my God, these are gross! she thought, gazing in disgust at the oversized man's tweed jacket she was wearing, over a crummy scratchy woollen dress and an apron. *An apron!* Through the jacket sleeve she checked that her watch was still there. And she had her Docs and her army rucksack.

"How did you manage to steal that?" Catherine was pointing at it.

"It's mine!" Rosie was aggrieved at the accusation.

Catherine laughed. "Not unless you've joined the army. You'd better come inside. You don't want to be caught with that. Anyway, it's freezing out here."

Catherine had no coat and her toes were a strange mottled purple. The ground was coated with ice. The poor girl's feet must be stuck to the pavement.

"What happened to your hair?"

Rosie raised a hand and felt the spiky growth and Catherine went on, "Fleas, I suppose. "Mother says shaving your head is the only way to get rid of fleas. Do you have any scabs?"

Rosie swallowed her indignation and shook her head. Catherine was comforting, "I suppose you think you hair is horrible, but don't worry, it'll soon grow."

Rosie gritted her teeth and said nothing. She thought her hair was cool and did fierce battle with Mom and Miss Graham to keep it that way. But it was obvious from Catherine's sympathy that a twelve-year-old in 1920 would rather drop dead than have a cropped head.

I wish she could see Dolores O'Riordan, Rosie thought.

She followed her new friend up the steps. Inside, the stench was overpowering and she nearly fainted.

What was it? A smell of old cooking – cabbage mixed with rotten eggs – and sweating armpits. Once again she gripped her nose and tried not to breathe, her eyes watering with the effort.

The house vibrated with sound. People clattered down the stairs. Doors opened, voices called. It was much noisier than the street. How many lived here?

"We're on the second floor," Catherine said, "Be careful, some of the banisters are gone and a few of the stairs are rotten."

Still clutching her nose, Rosie kept close to the wall. Their progress was slow enough. Neighbours kept stopping Catherine to enquire about her mother and time after time almost the exact same conversation followed: "Oh, she had to go into Jervis Street hospital," Catherine would say. "No, we don't think it's TB, but she has to have tests. The doctor thinks she just needs a rest after the flu. I'll be visiting her on Wednesday night."

And each neighbour would say in almost the same words, "Please God she'll be fine. Now you be sure to knock on my door if you need anything. And come for your tea any time. Any time, d'you hear! And if you get sight or sound of a Crossley lorry, you're to race into our place 'cos no one is safe with the Tans."

How poor they looked, Rosie thought. The women wore shawls and their faces were old. Their dry straggly hair was tied back in a bun. They reminded her of the women on the cover of Gran's book. Careworn. Most of them were missing teeth and those they did have moved independently when they talked.

The men were more confident, more energetic, the younger ones taking the stairs three at a time. But their clothes were frayed and mismatched and their collarless shirts had seen better days decades ago. You'd think everyone was dressed from a jumble sale and all of them

– men and women – were shorter and skinnier than people from her own time.

"Who's your pal?" one of the men asked Catherine, and without waiting for an answer went on, "I do hope Miss, you're not bringing any fleas, scabies or ringworm into this magnificent palace!"

Rosie's watery eyes glared at him, "I habn't god addy of dose dings," she said.

The man laughed, "Is she a Chinee," he asked Catherine, "and why is she holding her nose? Does she think it's going to fall off?"

Furious, Rosie let her nose go and opened her mouth to say something but the smell was so awful she gagged instead.

Catherine opened the door to the room and Rosie tried not to shudder. Plaster was peeling from the walls and ceiling. The tall window was covered in grime. In the huge grate old ashes emphasised the icy cold. There were two mattresses in the corner, covered with what looked like a heap of rags. A small splintered table and two rickety chairs stood by the fireplace. Apart from a dingy cupboard this was all the furniture. The floor was bare with gaps between the boards. The only relic of past glory was the elegant marble fireplace and mantelpiece. Rosie took in the framed photo of Catherine's father on the mantel beside the Virgin Mary statue and the picture of the Sacred Heart. Below this was a small red glass containing an unlit candle.

How could anyone bear this? Rosie thought. How was she going to bear it, even for a week? The smell, the cold, the grim room! It was horrible. Miserable, she wished she'd never come back. There could be no joy in

41

this place. The people looked like goblins with their skinny bodies and gapped mouths. She thought of central heating, blazing fires, warm delicious food and almost wept. This was hell, only freezing.

Then Catherine turned and smiled. "Would you like some milk?" Speechless, Rosie nodded. The girl fetched two cracked mugs and a jug from the cupboard and poured. It tasted different, thicker and richer than the milk at home.

"Can I have some more?"

Catherine was troubled. "I'm sorry, there isn't any more." She hesitated, then said, "There's no food at all!" Her face reddened and she bowed her head.

"Oh, I nearly forgot," Rosie said, eyes alight, "I brought some food with me. I knew you wouldn't have much."

She hauled the rucksack on to the table, unaware of Catherine's astonished face, then halted in her tracks when her new friend said, "What do you mean, you *knew*? How could you *know*?"

"I don't know why I said that." Rosie put a hand to her head and Catherine stared at her, baffled.

"Anyway, have a look at this." Keeping a firm grip through the material on the camera, Rosie upended the rest of the contents on to the table which creaked from the shock of unaccustomed weight. Her dark eyes widened and Catherine gasped with delight. "Oh, smashing! Terrific!"

Rosie could not help beaming at her joy. "Cool!" she said.

"Who cares? It's food, isn't it? Anyway we can always heat some up."

"No, I meant – "

"What's this . . . and this?" Catherine was examining the peanut butter and the muesli.

42

Rosie explained. "You could try the peanut butter now, if you have a knife." Opening a drawer under the table, Catherine passed her a bockety knife, the handle half gone. Rosie managed to cut the defrosted loaf and plaster it with peanut butter. Catherine's mouth was already open and she tore into the bread, devouring it. Rosie's mouth was open too – with amazement. She had never seen such starvation! Gathering her wits she prepared a second, then a third and fourth slice until all the bread and peanut butter were gone. Then Catherine carefully gathered the crumbs into the palm of her hand and ate them. At last she sat back.

"That was beautiful," she said dreamily. "That was the most beautiful thing that ever happened to me."

"Oh . . . good." For once Rosie was speechless. She quite liked peanut butter, but it didn't send her into ecstasy. And if Catherine ate at this rate there'd be nothing left in half an hour. But her new friend was full. "What are these?" She was examining her Nike air runners.

"Aren't they deadly!" Rosie said, fingering the transparent plastic bubble in the heel. She saw Catherine's puzzlement and amended, "Massive. They're massive."

Catherine was not enlightened. "I suppose they *are* very big," she said. "Do they belong to a man? What are they for?" She held one for closer inspection and Rosie snatched it back.

"They are only size five. They're mine and they're cool with jeans – " One look at Catherine's face and she gave up. "Well, I think they're beautiful," she finished.

Her friend was not convinced. "If you say so, but I'd prefer button boots any day."

"Then you can have my boots." As soon as she

thought of it, Rosie started unlacing. "And take the spare pair of socks too." She shoved them across the table.

"I can't . . . you can't . . ."

Rosie had never met anyone her own age who didn't like Docs, but then neither had she met anyone who preferred button boots to Nike air runners.

"Do you not like them?"

Catherine swallowed, "Not like them!" she said, "not like them! I *love* them. They're the berries!" She clutched them to her chest and once more Rosie was aware of a depth of feeling she did not understand.

"As long as you don't kiss them," she muttered.

The boots were far too big and Catherine stuffed newspaper down the toes while Rosie put on the runners.

"We'll have to give some of the food to the neighbours. Or maybe we could just have a party and invite everyone. What do you think, Rosie?"

Rosie was speechless. She had just hauled a sack of food across more than seventy-five years into a starving home and the nitwit wanted to give a party with it. She, Rosie, would go hungry for the week. Had the girl no brains?

"Why would we do that?" she said as soon as she could speak. "We'll have nothing for ourselves."

"Sure we'll have to share!" Catherine was adamant. "Everyone does. The neighbours have been so good to Mother and me since Father went away. Mrs Hennessey sends us up pigs' feet and fishhead stew whenever she can. Mrs Reilly'd give you her last crust of bread, and Mr Dempsey . . ."

Rosie felt faint and wondered fleetingly how Gran hadn't been killed off in childhood, poisoned by fishhead stew. Were the heads left in it, floating around staring at their victim? Were you meant to eat them? She did not want to know. More than ever she was reluctant to give away the food, but Catherine was already planning.

"We'll ask Mrs Hennessey can we have the hooley in her room. That way Lilian can be there. Lilian's her daughter and my friend. She has the flu and her mother won't let her out. Come on – we'll ask now!"

Before she could object, Catherine was flying out of the room, gripped with excitement. At random Rosie picked up the tea bags and stuffed them back into the rucksack. Swiftly, she took off her digital watch and zipped it into a side pocket. On her trip to the fifties the watch had aroused suspicions with its date, time zones and calculator. It could only have a worse effect in 1920.

Then she followed Catherine, her man's jacket flapping awkwardly around her, the sleeves half a foot too long.

In the room below Catherine was already explaining about the food. "Rosie brought it. Don't ask her where she got it. She's after losing her memory but I bet it belonged to the Tans 'cos it's in an army kit-bag."

Mrs Hennessey rested a hand on her shoulder. "Would you slow down, child. You have my head battered with your excitement." She looked up at Rosie and for a long moment they stared at each other. This was her great-grandmother and the family resemblance was striking. The same brown eyes she and Mom and Gran had and the same heart-shaped face. Mrs Hennessey had fair hair, like hers. Gazing at the woman Rosie knew what she herself would look like in her thirties. Perhaps she would be taller, less pale and tired, but there would be no other major differences.

She wondered if this family similarity ran through time. Was there someone in the eighteenth century who bore her likeness? Someone in the 21st who would look the same?

"Who are you?" Mrs Hennessey whispered, "You look just like Lilian!"

Startled, Catherine examined her friend. "No she doesn't," she said. "Her hair's completely different, and her mouth."

Rosie smiled, white teeth gleaming, and her great-grandmother slowly nodded. "It's a trick of the light," she said. "For a moment, standing there in the shadow of the doorway, I almost thought you *were* Lilian. Best come in properly and meet her. Then we can talk about this hooley."

The Hennessey room was neat. Mattresses were piled up in one corner. The floor was swept and a tiny fire was lighting. On the one collapsing couch, a girl her own age was snoozing.

"Wake up, Lilian. You have visitors." Mrs Hennessey shook her daughter and the girl opened her eyes. She stared at Rosie who looked away, hoping Lilian would not see their resemblance. Anxious to divert attention she asked, "Where are the three boys?"

"Their father has taken them off to the docks," Mrs Hennessey said. "There's a coal ship in and they've been promised work. Just as well the schools are closed for the week. With the bit they earn, maybe we can help with the hooley."

Although Rosie was listening to Mrs Hennessey, she was conscious of Lilian's stare. She turned to smile but the girl did not smile back.

"How did you know I have brothers?" Her tone was hostile.

46

Catherine too looked puzzled and waited for an answer.

"Lilian!" Mrs Hennessey was embarrassed. "Don't mind her, Rosie. She's still not well. And as for you, Miss, don't be so rude. Why wouldn't she know about your brothers? Wouldn't she have seen and heard them clattering out of this room a few minutes ago? She'd have to be stone deaf to miss them!"

About to object, Lilian was interrupted by Catherine, who was still excited by the party. "We're having a bash," she told her, "down here, so that you'll be able to come."

At last Lilian smiled and her mother said, "I'd best go and have a look at this wonderful food."

The second Mrs Hennessey pushed open the door, she screeched, almost giving Rosie a heart attack. "Bowsies!" she roared. Then Rosie saw them. Two huge rats on the table, nibbling away at the chocolate. Mrs Hennessey promptly unbuckled her shoe and slammed it down on the table, missing the rats who pretended nothing was wrong.

"Oh, I'll get you, you thieving vultures. Ignore me at your peril." Smartly she whacked both rats and they scattered, squealing.

"The rotten scavengers. They'd leave nothing." She eyed the chocolate. "Could I take a piece?" Rosie nodded, embarrassed by the tentative question. Her great-grandmother broke off the gnawed squares and popped them into her mouth, madly biting and swallowing. "Ah, lovely," she sighed. "The Brits know how to feed themselves. This is beautiful stuff. And just look at the way the rashers are done up!" She studied the vacuum packed bacon and the rest of the food, item by item. Then she said, "Please God, Mr Hennessey and

47

the boys'll make a good few bob. We'll get a good fire going and a few bottles of stout in. Mr Dempsey can bring his gramophone. This place is in sore need of a good time."

"Will you mind the stuff, Mrs H?" Catherine said, "our cupboard doesn't lock and the rats might get at it."

"Indeedin I will." Holding up her apron with one hand, Mrs Hennessey swept the contents of the table into it. "If those bowsies come near this, I'll catch and cook them and we'll eat them as well!" She laughed merrily until she saw Rosie's dismayed face. "Dear God, child, I'm only joking. Tomorrow night for the hooley then."

When she was gone Rosie looked at the empty table. "What are we going to eat now? You've given everything away." She was almost wailing, but Catherine was confident. "William will have something for us. He's my friend and he works in the Gresham. I want to invite him tomorrow night anyway. We can call on him now."

"Why don't you invite the whole street?" Rosie muttered, but not loud enough for the other girl to hear. Catherine was quite capable of thinking this was a wonderful idea.

Rosie followed her once more out the door.

Chapter 5

FROM HER vantage point near the Gresham, Rosie stared down O'Connell Street in consternation.

What on earth had happened to the GPO?

It looked as though it had been hit by a bomb. The whole front was blackened and large chunks were missing from the balustrade above. Through the front pillars she could see the windows and doors had been boarded up.

Racking her brains she remembered one of Miss Graham's history lessons: "During Easter 1916, British naval guns on the Liffey bombarded the GPO which Pearse and his men had taken over. When the revolutionaries surrendered, the building was a smoking ruin and was not restored to its former glory for many years."

Surveying the rest of the street, Rosie caught her breath. In the winter sunlight the shop window awnings had something of the gaiety of summer with their colourful stripes. The street looked wider, maybe because it wasn't chock-a-block with buses and cars. There were no traffic lights. Horses and carts and the odd motor-car meandered up and down the cobblestones without apparent order. Electric trams clanged their bells.

Pedestrians ambled. Cyclists were leisurely. Everyone except children wore hats. The street lights were old-fashioned, some like lanterns, others delicate globes framed by wrought iron, high on the lamp standards.

In the middle of the street was Nelson's Pillar, rising higher than the rooftops. Rosie recalled what Mom had told her: "Inside there was a spiral staircase to a viewing balcony. From there you could look across the city. One rag day a Trinity student climbed right up Nelson himself and put a potty on his head, or so people said."

Mom had never climbed the pillar. "If I'd known it was going to be blown up, I'd certainly have done it. I always meant to. Then it was too late."

Catherine followed Rosie's gaze, puzzled. "What are you staring at? Come on, let's get off Sackville Street. We'd better call on William before he gets too busy to see us."

Following her down North Earl Street, Rosie was goggle-eyed. She had never seen such poor people, so many children without shoes, wearing an extraordinary mishmash of ill fitting clothes. One man had his coat tied together with twine. She nearly fell over at the sight of a boy, not much younger than herself. "Why is he wearing a skirt?" she nudged Catherine. "Why wouldn't he, if he has no trousers?" Her friend's logic was unanswerable.

Down the alley they went and sidled in the back entrance of the grand hotel. A young fellow sweeping the kitchen floor looked up and grinned at Catherine. He made a mock charge at her with the sweeping brush. She tried to seize it and a good-natured battle followed. It ended when the boy tripped over the brush and went flying into a tall man who had just appeared through the door.

He was the most impressive-looking man Rosie had ever seen, like a prince or a general, she thought. Dressed in a dark red uniform with gold buttons and épaulettes, he stood, silent, magnificent, arms folded, eyebrows raised while the boy picked himself off the floor.

"Sorry, Mr Callaghan." He was still gasping from his impact with the magnificent person's chest.

"So you should be, trying to gallop over me like a horse. You'd think I was a maggot to be pounded into the ground."

"Oh, no, Mister Callaghan, I wouldn't hurt a poor maggot!"

"Oho! You'd spare a maggot, would you, but you wouldn't worry about me? Is that the way to treat your superior?"

Since any answer would condemn him, the boy kept silent. He caught Rosie's eye and winked. She liked him at once. A tall fellow, his eyes gleamed with mischief and for all his respectful tone he looked as if he were on the verge of laughter. Mister Callaghan rocked on his heels and looked at the two girls.

"You young ladies should exercise a calming effect on William, not help him do the Charge of The Light Brigade all over again. These kitchens aren't meant for such shenanigans."

Rosie giggled nervously and Mr Callaghan frowned. She hastily coughed and was astonished to see him smile, the stern look replaced at once by kindliness.

"I was hoping you'd call," he said to Catherine. "A gentleman I know wishes to employ someone trustworthy to run errands. He is willing to pay quite well for a suitable person. I told him you must be consulted first and if agreeable I would make the introductions."

"Agreeable? Agreeable! Oh, Mister C, that is smashing!" Catherine was giving little jumps and Mr Callaghan looked pleased, "Then if you three will follow me into the recess, I shall bring Mr Foley to see you."

In the alcove off the kitchens, William pondered, "I don't know why I'm here. Mr Callaghan will hardly let me run errands with all the work I've to do."

Remembering the man's splendid uniform Rosie said, "Mister Callaghan must be a very high-up person."

"Oh indeed he is," William was earnest. "He's the hall porter and all the Boots have to answer to him."

"Isn't his uniform a bit over the top, then?" Rosie said, thinking Mr Callaghan looked like pictures she had seen of Prince Charles on his wedding day.

Mystified, William said, "Over the top of what?"

"A bit fancy," Rosie amended.

"It's not fancy enough!" The boy was indignant. "You should see the doorman at the *Sackville Picture House*. He looks like a Christmas tree in his uniform. Mister Callaghan says it's disgraceful. After all, the Gresham is a far more important establishment. So he's going to ask for gold fringes to be added and some tassels – " He stopped. A young man had entered the alcove.

"I'm Foley," he introduced himself, "now, who are you?" Catherine did the introductions and he looked keenly at Rosie. "Mr C didn't tell me about you."

"She's my pal," Catherine was firm. "She goes everywhere with me."

"But can she be trusted?"

Rosie's face darkened. She did not know what to make of Foley. He had the authority of a middle-aged man, yet she reckoned he wasn't much more than twenty. He was well-dressed, wearing a long, open, belted overcoat over a grey suit. His shirt had a high stiff collar and a neat tie. On his head a soft hat was tipped at a rakish angle. His eyes glittered like the cold sea.

"I don't care whether you trust me or not," Rosie said. "You can keep your stupid job!"

"No, he can't," Catherine was appalled. "She doesn't mean that, Mr Foley." She gave Rosie a dig. "We need the money, remember."

Foley smiled and Rosie noticed his eyes did not grow warmer. "I like your spirit," he told her, "you'll do. Now here's what I want!" He nodded at William, "You keep a watch on all male visitors to the hotel this week. When you've polished their boots, don't just leave them back outside the door. Knock. Make up some problem. Get a good description of the guest: height, age, appearance, accent. For that, you'll be paid one and six a day, in advance."

William beamed as Foley took some coins from his pocket.

"Hang on," Rosie said, "why's he got to spy on people? Why don't you do your own dirty work?"

Foley, in the act of handing the money to William, paused.

"Don't mind her!" The boy was raging, seeing his extra cash disappear. "You'd think she was a millionaire! I'll do your dirty work, Mister Foley. Rosie must be loopy."

"She's lost her memory," Catherine confided. "She probably got a bang on the head, though she says she didn't. But that'd explain why she's not the full shilling."

53

Foley looked doubtful, "This isn't a job for the weak-minded! I'm not sure she should be working for me. What if her nerve goes?"

Rosie, caught between the desire to tell Foley again what he could do with his job and fury at Catherine for implying she was mad, opened and shut her mouth, spluttering. Catherine patted her arm soothingly. "Oh, she's very brave, Mister Foley. Why, she robbed a Tan's kit-bag."

Foley's eyes widened, impressed. "What was in it?" he said.

"Food. So you see you needn't worry about her."

Before he could reply, Rosie butted in, finding her voice at last. "I still want to know what's going on. And you're not to talk about me as if I'm not here. It makes me feel like an idiot!"

About to say something, William clutched his ankle instead. "Ouch! What was that for, Catherine?" But Catherine looked innocent.

Foley leaned forward, addressing Rosie. "The people I want you to 'spy on', as you call it, are criminals of the worst kind. They have harmed a lot of people and must be brought to justice." His voice was low and earnest and they could not doubt his conviction. "And if you want nothing to do with the work I have to offer, tell me now and no harm done." He was looking at Rosie for an answer.

"Say yes!" groaned Catherine.

Remembering the empty cupboards and cheerless room, Rosie thought hard. "Is it dangerous work?" she stalled, and without hesitation Foley said, "It could be. I'd do it myself but my face is known and I'd come under suspicion. You have a better chance, being kids, but yes, there could be trouble."

At once Rosie's eyes gleamed and she nodded. "OK. Yes."

Immediately Foley gave William his money. "You better get on with your work, lad, before the powers that be come looking for you."

When he'd gone, Foley's instructions to the girls were rapid. "I want you to go across to Morehampton Road and locate the address of a man called Donald McClean."

"How do we do that?" Rosie was sceptical. "Do we knock on every door and ask for him?"

Foley went white. "I hope you won't be so stupid! You do that and McClean is bound to hear about it. He'll know you're spying. I told you, he's a villain. He could kill you without hesitation! Do you understand?" He was deadly serious. Rosie swallowed and nodded.

He went on, "He and others are in league with the men William is looking out for. They are trying to cheat friends of mine out of a great sum of money."

"These friends of yours," Rosie said, "are they business men?"

"In a way. They are good men. My job is to stop McClean and his kind."

Studying his intense face, Rosie was troubled. "What do you mean, 'stop them'?"

Foley's eyes were hooded. "Bring them to justice, that's all. You're not having more doubts?"

She thought of courts of law and prison sentences for villainous men and was comforted. After all what else could he mean? She knew Catherine would take the job even if she didn't and could be days looking for McClean. Without her company Rosie would have nothing to do. She might even lose track of her and, anyway, Foley made it sound so exciting!

Time to stop dithering.

"No more doubts," Rosie said. "It's cool." They stared at her. "Straight up," she said, "Everything's A OK!" God, did they not speak English?

"It's the blow on the head . . ." both Foley and Catherine announced simultaneously and the three of them burst out laughing. For a moment Foley looked like a schoolboy and Rosie found it easier to like him.

"Two shillings a day, each. What do you say?"

"Four shillings! Mr Foley, that is smashing!" Catherine was ecstatic.

Rosie calculated. An old shilling was worth five pence modern. That made twenty pence a day between them. Hardly the Lotto, but as long as Catherine was happy.

"And sixpence for extras," Foley added, watching Rosie's face. "You'll have to take the tram."

"Yes, and can we hire a basket car from Mister Weinberger?" Catherine asked, her face lighting up at the idea. "That way we can go tugging for scrap. No one will think it strange then if we call at different doors. And we might make a few more bob."

"Great plan. Really clever." Foley's praise was warm and Rosie felt almost envious of her friend.

They arranged to meet him again next day in the hotel at half eleven in the morning. "And remember, not a word to anyone else. This is a secret between us and William and Mister Callaghan."

After he'd left they waited for William to tell him what happened. His face grew anxious when he heard. "If McClean is a villain it's not fair to send two girls after him."

Rosie bristled. "Girls are just as brave as boys," she snapped.

56

"But not as strong, or are you planning to knock him unconscious with one blow from your huge fist?" William asked sarcastically.

"I won't need to because I'm cunning," Rosie stated. "Anyway, who are you to talk? You're a beanstalk."

"He is not," Catherine was outraged at the insult to her friend. "You should see him in a ruggy-up. He'll take on anyone. Why are you so mean to him?"

"I'm not. I'm just saying girls are as good as boys." Rosie was indignant but outnumbered.

"'Course they are," William said. "Just not as strong."

"Gorillas are strong too. That doesn't make them better. Or maybe you'd like to be a gorilla."

William looked hurt and Rosie decided to drop it. There was an awkward silence, then Catherine rescued the situation. "I nearly forgot. We're having a hooley tomorrow night. Will you come?"

William beamed. "It's my night off. I'll be there." Then his face fell, "I can't get you any food today. Mr Doyle, the manager, is on the prowl and if he caught me I'd get the sack."

Catherine showed him her money. "Foley gave us this. We can buy food. We've to meet him here tomorrow, so we'll see you then."

Leaving the Gresham, Catherine led the way through a warren of lanes to a dilapidated shed with the sign:

WEINBERGER: SCRAP MERCHANT
WANTED
OLD IRON OLD CLOTHES ALL JUNK

A large man was blocking the entrance, smoking a corona cigar and gazing genially at the world. He wore a trilby hat and an overcoat so heavy it seemed to Rosie he was bowed under its weight.

"And for you young ladies, what can I do?" His accent was slightly foreign.

"We want to hire a basket car, Mr Weinberger."

"Ahah! And are you selling or only collecting?" The words were clipped, since the cigar remained clenched between his teeth.

"We've nothing to sell, Mr Weinberger."

He smiled brilliantly then and, removing the corona, blew a perfect smoke ring.

"Young ladies, I have something for you to sell. Some beautiful statues. You ask sixpence for them, then you keep a penny. What do you think? Good, yes?"

Catherine was overjoyed, but Rosie was paying no attention, thoroughly engrossed by the scene behind the large man.

Inside the shed two long tables were piled high with what looked like rags and junk. Six women at each table were working at breakneck speed sorting the rubbish into various heaps. Mr Weinberger followed her gaze. "When you come back," he said, "You make your choice of these wares. They are magnificent. For you of course there is a discount. What better way to spend your profit, hey?"

The man was serious! Rosie managed not to laugh.

"Oh thank you, Mr Weinberger, you are so kind!" Catherine was utterly sincere.

He waved the cigar expansively. "No need for thanks. But you, I think, are feeling the cold and would like a coat now, yes? And no charge." Catherine's eyes lit up.

"Then follow, please, young ladies."

He led them to a corner and from an unsorted heap,

deftly selected a woman's black coat. Eagerly Catherine put it on. Rosie was horrified. The thing was revolting. Not only was it enormous and grimy, but one sleeve was half-ripped at the shoulder and the colour made Catherine look dead.

Suddenly conscious of her own outsize jacket, Rosie felt rage. We look like circus clowns, she thought. Right eejits! Silly and ridiculous. Nobody respectable would want to have anything to do with us.

Seeing her face, Catherine said, "It's very warm, Rosie, and I'm freezing."

Tight-lipped, her friend nodded.

"It's too big for you." Mr Weinberger was gruff. He too had caught the look in Rosie's eyes. "Let me give you something better."

This time he went through the pile carefully, at last picking out a lady's jacket. It was red, waisted and hip-length. There was a big hole in each pocket, but otherwise the coat was perfect. Best of all the colour brought Catherine's pale features to life.

"That's really cool," Rosie smiled. "Lovely."

Mr Weinberger laughed with satisfaction, "Your friend, she is difficult to please!" He chucked Catherine under the chin. "But now she approves. Let us get the statues and the basket car and then you do your tugging."

The statues were truly awful. The Virgin Mary and The Sacred Heart were made of chalk and badly painted. Rosie thought The Sacred Heart could do with a transplant. In some cases the heart was only a red blob and in others it seemed to be closer to his shoulder than his chest. Most of the statues' faces were blank. Mr Weinberger lovingly placed twelve of each into the basket car, a wicker contraption that looked like a large bucket on two wheels, with a bar across the top for pushing or tugging. Charging them threepence hire, he waved them goodbye.

As they made their way to Sackville Street and the tram terminus, the Angelus bells rang out louder than Rosie ever remembered hearing them.

An army lorry screeched past. "Why on earth do they do that? They'd give you a heart attack!" It was about the fifth lorry Rosie had seen that morning, every one of them driven the same way.

"You mean the Crossleys," Catherine said. "Sure if they went any slower, they'd be fired at."

Rosie halted in her tracks, nervously looking around for gunmen.

"What are you doing?" Catherine asked. "You're not going to see any snipers. They don't go around waving their guns. The time to worry is if the Crossleys slow down or stop. Then we have to get out of the way fast!" Puzzled, she looked at Rosie, "Anyone would think you were a stranger, the way you behave. How is it you can remember your name but nothing else?"

Rosie struggled for a plausible answer, but in the end could only say, "I don't know." Seeing her worried face, Catherine was immediately sympathetic. "It'll be all right, Rosie. You'll get better."

Rosie studied the way the trams moved, attached to the overhead electric wires by the slimmest of metal rods on the roof. They climbed aboard a tram with 'Donnybrook' written in large letters on the front and back nameplates.

The basket car was put on the motorman's platform behind for an extra threepence.

"Are we going soon?" Catherine asked the driver.

He shook his head. "I've a fellow's lunch to drop off at the Munster and Leinster bank and a parcel at the Hammam hotel. After that we're off."

Intrigued, Rosie said, "Is the driver some sort of postman?"

"Your head *is* bad," Catherine sighed, "The trams only deliver parcels, not letters."

"Oh that's right," her friend muttered and risked another question. "Why does this tram have blue diamonds on it while the one over there has a green shamrock?"

"So's you know where you're going, of course!"

"But it says where we're going in huge letters!"

"Well, that's no good if you can't read, dopey!"

Rosie looked around her, half-smiling half-disgusted at a notice on the side:

NO SPITTING GENTLEMEN, PLEASE

She had a close view of Nelson's Pillar through the back window. Cool! Maybe they could go up there. That would be something to remember.

The day had grown duller and a chill east wind made her shiver. She looked at Sackville Street, at the women in long skirts and the men in trilbys, at the old-fashioned motor cars and shop awnings. All of a sudden she had a sense of being trapped in time, like figures in a sepia photograph.

She thought of the adventure ahead, of Foley and McClean and felt afraid. What if something went wrong? What if being from the future didn't mean she was invincible? What if she never got back?

Her eyes focused on a figure outside the GPO. It was Foley. The collar of his overcoat was up and the brim of his hat pulled low so that his face was shaded and sinister. Lifting his head he caught Rosie staring at him. He did not move or smile, but locked his eyes on hers.

The tram began to move, so that Rosie had to turn to keep him in view. With an effort she broke the connection and sat back, trembling.

Chapter 6

"FILTHY BEGGARS! Go away at once or I'll call the polis!"

The maid who opened the door at number 100 was definitely hostile. Rosie shrank into her man's jacket, but Catherine was unabashed. "We're not begging, Missus. These are lovely statues and they're only sixpence each." She proffered a Sacred Heart for inspection.

"It's disgusting!" said the maid and would have slammed the door only Catherine's foot prevented her.

"Oh, dear God, what a thing to say!" Catherine blessed herself dramatically, "may the Lord forgive you!" Her voice was pious and she raised her eyes to heaven. Rosie looked at her with great interest.

"Forgive me for what?" the maid snapped.

"Blasphemy!" Catherine's tones were sorrowful. "These statues have been blessed in Lourdes. How could you call the Sacred Heart and his mother disgusting? You're after putting your immortal soul in danger." Rosie hadn't been so entertained for a long time and did not know how Catherine managed to keep serious. To her astonishment the maid's face became pale and anxious.

"I didn't know they were blessed," she was almost apologetic, "and anyway I've three statues already."

"But none of them consecrated with Lourdes water!" Catherine went in for the kill. "And these are the only twelve left in Dublin."

The maid was impressed but still hesitant, "How much did you say they were?"

"Sevenpence each to you. That's a special price because you'll give them a good home to make up for your terrible insults."

"A minute ago you said they were sixpence!"

"I couldn't have. It'd show no respect for God and his blessed mother if I gave them away for that. These are powerful statues, Missus, and if you say a decade of the sorrowful mysteries sure they'll answer all your requests."

"All right so, I'll take one of each." The maid was hooked, foraging deep in her apron for money. When the exchange was done, she looked at the statues, dismayed. "They have no faces," she said, "and the Sacred Heart's heart is nearly on his arm!" But Catherine was already pulling the basket car down the garden. "I told you they were special," she called back as Rosie hastily followed her. "They've no faces because they are mysterious beings. And God can have his heart anywhere he likes. He's all-powerful."

Rosie was full of admiration, "You were brilliant," she said. "Lourdes water was a masterstroke." Catherine stopped at once, outraged. "I wasn't lying. Mr Weinberger says all his statues are blessed in Lourdes. I might have exaggerated a bit about how many were left, but that doesn't count."

"Does he have a lot of statues?"

"Millions."

"Lourdes must be running out of holy water, so," Rosie muttered.

She noticed how elegant the houses in this area were compared to North Great Georges Street. Set back from the road, their gardens neat and trim, paintwork spotless, rich drapes in the windows. Every door was opened by a maid. Skilfully Catherine sold all the statues, sometimes asking as much as eightpence. And when she'd got on friendly terms with the maid she'd enquire, "Is the master of the house in?"

Mostly she got a straight reply, "No, Mr Fitzgerald, or Mr Jones, or Mr Whoever, is not at home today."

In the garden of number 117, a boy somewhat younger than themselves was throwing a ball in the air. He looked bored. Seeing the girls, he came over to the gate.

"Who are you?" he said, "What are your names?" Rosie noticed how warm he looked in his gloves, scarf and a woollen cap with ear flaps. His accent was English and quite posh, but he had a cheeky face and smiling blue eyes.

Catherine was not inclined to be friendly and drew herself up. "My name is Priscilla Potts," she said, much to her friend's astonishment, "and this is Gertrude Gumley – known as Gertie."

Rosie gasped.

The boy opened the gate and held out a hand, "How do you do, Gertie and Priscilla – or should I say 'Prissy' for short? I'm Tommy Smith."

Hastily Catherine wiped her palms on her skirt before shaking the boy's gloved hand. Rosie did not. She was staring at his baggy trousers that fastened just below the knee, where his big thick socks began. "What do you call those?" she pointed.

"Why, this is my knickerbocker suit," he said. "Isn't

it smart?" Rosie was too polite to snigger. It was a good name, she thought.

The boy was examining the basket car. "Can I have a go in that?" he said.

"It's not a pram!" Catherine told him. "You're too big for it."

"Bet I'm not," he said, "I'll give you sixpence to push me down to the corner and back as fast as you can go."

"Done!" said Catherine, tipping the car forward on its two wheels. The boy sat in, his legs dangling over the rim.

"You look like an overgrown baby!" Rosie said.

"Don't care." He gave them the sixpence. "Now mind, both of you must push, hell for leather. One, two, three. Go, Gertie, go!"

Catherine and Rosie looked at each other grimly. With one accord they pushed up their sleeves, grabbed a handle each and did a mad gallop down the path, with Tommy Smith roaring encouragement, "Push, Prissy! Go, Gertie, go!" At the corner they stopped so abruptly he nearly fell out, then they did a U-turn and raced back to his garden gate. Tommy climbed out beaming. "That was fun!" he said. "Does either of you want a go?" Before they could decide a cross voice called from the front door, "Master Tommy, come in here at once!"

"Darn it." He frowned and pushed through the gate, dragging his way up the path. A maid stood there, arms akimbo. The boy turned to wave, "Thanks, Gertie. Thanks, Prissy."

When he'd gone in the maid glared at the girls. "Ruffians!" she shouted before slamming the door.

"Why did you give him false names?" Rosie said.

"I always do that with posh people," Catherine told her, "then if you sell them something they don't like

65

later, they don't know who you are to come after you and they can never give the polis your right name."

"But he was nice," Rosie said. "He wouldn't have done us any harm."

Her friend grinned. "He *was* a good sport. I thought he'd hate it when we nearly tipped him out."

"And by the way, next time call me something better than 'Gertie Gumley'," Rosie told her. "You'd think I was simple with a name like that."

"Yes . . . well, I thought it suited you all right!" Catherine grinned.

"Huh! And I suppose 'Prissy' made you sound like a genius!"

They were just about to move on from number 117 when a young postman stopped them. He was out of breath. "Do us a favour. Deliver these for me. Have to meet my girl, see, and I'm late as it is. This is my last house." He winked and pushed the post into their hands, striding on up the road.

Once he disappeared, Catherine studied the four envelopes and caught her breath. "Two for Captain Donald Louis McClean," she said, "one for Mr Cadlow and one for Mr T H Smith – he must be Tommy's father. Do you think we should keep these for Foley?"

"No, I don't!" Rosie was horrified.

"But McClean is a villain. He's dangerous. You heard what Foley said."

"Maybe Foley is the villain!"

Catherine considered. "No, I don't think so . . . he's a generous man. He didn't have to give us so much money to do the job. And he's honest. He told us straight out it could be dangerous." But her friend's face was stubborn and Catherine sighed. "Look, Rosie, Mr Foley's life could be in danger. If these other two –

Cadlow and Smith – are in the same house as McClean, they could be villains too. So let's at least open the letters. We can deliver them afterwards. No one will know we've looked at them."

Before Rosie could say another word, Catherine was gone, hurrying around the corner. She caught up on her, seated on a bench beneath a tree. The road was empty apart from a carter who had stopped some way down to let his horse drink from a stone trough.

Already Catherine was working on the envelope flap with the blade of a small penknife. "Sometimes they're not properly stuck down." She frowned, biting her lip with concentration. When the flap was three-quarters open, she stopped, slipped a finger inside and eased out the letter. Opening out the sheet, she read:

Monday 15th November

Captain McClean,

Everything is in order. Your presence is undetected. This time we shall ruin their lives. They will be wiped out. Be ready next week. Contact will be made as soon as the day is settled. Tell Smith and Cadlow good luck. You could not have finer, more steady comrades for this enterprise. I shall play my own part.

God go with you.

For King and country.

WF Newbury.

"*They will be wiped out.*" Catherine murmured. "That probably means Foley and his friends. McClean *must* be a villain, then."

Rosie wasn't so sure. There was something odd about the letter. Did villains say, "God go with you," or "For King and country"? Yet W F Newbury certainly wanted to ruin people's lives. She sighed, "You might be right, but I can't make head nor tail of it."

Opening the second letter to McClean with the same infinite caution, Catherine read:

My Dearest Love,

Two days gone and you are missed already. I wear your locket always and think of you constantly. How proud I am of your fine courage. Yesterday your mother called and of course we talked of nothing but you; how brave and wild you were as a boy and your great sense of fun. She said you could always make her smile, even after you'd done something recklessly dangerous.

You haven't changed, Donald, and though I sometimes wish our lives were different, I would not alter you for the world. I would tell you to take care but I may as well tell the oceans to cease moving.

I hope you will be home soon.

God watch over you.

With all my love,

M.

"*She* doesn't think he's a villain," Rosie said.

"No . . . we won't tell Foley about this . . . I don't think we need to open any more. After all, it's McClean he asked about."

Just before they got back to 117, Catherine licked the flaps and pressed them down. "I hope he doesn't notice they're not too sticky." Halfway up the path they were surprised when the door opened and a man came out. "Have either of you seen the postman?" he barked, bristling with impatience.

"Oh, he asked us to leave in some letters because he's very late today."

"Did he indeed?"

Rosie thought there was something familiar about his eyes. He was tall and dark-haired, with a trim beard. She did not understand her sense of recognition, certain she'd never seen him before.

Fuming, he went on about the postman, "Good-for-nothing malingerer! Needs a thrashing." His grey eyes were cold, glittering with anger. Of course! He reminded her of Foley. They had exactly the same icy expression.

He almost snatched the envelopes from Catherine, stuffing Cadlow's and Smith's into his pocket. They need not have worried, he was too impatient to notice any tampering.

Glancing at the handwriting, he tore open the one from M first and read it over and over.

When he finally looked up he was smiling and for a second, Rosie could see the mischievous boy described in the letter. "Sorry for snapping at you two. Bit on edge these days." Then he opened Newbury's letter. His frown returned and he sighed. Turning on his heels, he waved a dismissal and went indoors.

"After we pay Mr Weinberger for the statues, we're left with five shillings and ninepence, including what Mr Foley gave us." They were on the tram home and Catherine was busy doing her sums.

"Is that good?" Rosie was looking out the window, half-dreaming."

"Are you mental? Of course it's good! Some grown men don't get as much for a day's work!"

Mr Weinberger was well pleased. "I add you to my list of salespeople," he said, "If you can sell these statues you can sell your great-great-granny."

"But she's dead!" Catherine said.

"Exactly. An impossible task. But today you achieved the impossible. So many hundreds of my statues sitting in the warehouse and you, I think, are the ones to get rid of them for me. Yes? Tomorrow?"

"We can't." Catherine said, "Tomorrow we have to work for someone else."

He sighed. "So much in demand. But not surprising. You come back to me when you are available. Yes? My statues will be waiting."

Catherine was full of energy on the way home. "I can't believe it!" she said. "Last week I had no work. Mr Weinberger said I was too young to go tugging on my own. It's you, Rosie. You've brought me luck. Today I have two jobs and that boy Tommy gave us sixpence. What is it you always say for something good? It's cold!"

"Cool," Rosie muttered, struggling to keep up with her companion. She was so tired. "Will you stop jogging!" she snapped, exhausted.

"Stop what?" Catherine turned around and for diversion skipped along backwards. "Tell me if there's a lamppost in the way," she said.

Rosie glared at her, "Will you slow down!"

She was ignored. "There isn't a lamppost, "she said carefully, "but there is a cart-horse blocking the path and he's doing something rather disgusting."

"Ha, Ha!" The prancing figure in front continued her antics.

"No, really – "

"Aaagh!" It was too late. Catherine's boots squelched into a large soft smelly mess while Rosie neatly side-stepped on to the road.

Ten minutes later, when Catherine had cleaned her boots with a mixture of grass and old newspaper and was

70

ponging only a little, they were on their way again, this time at a normal pace. "You don't expect to find a horse in the middle of the path," Catherine grumbled. "What on earth was he doing there?"

"It's obvious from the smell on your boots what he was doing there," Rosie sniffed exaggeratedly. "Actually, his owner got off the cart and went into the shop. The horse was following and stopped for a toilet break."

"Stupid animal!"

Rosie, who had been silently fascinated all day by the amount of dung-heaps said, "Maybe horses should wear nappies!" Then they both got a fit of giggles and forgot their irritations.

Stopping at a corner shop they bought bread and milk, some beef dripping and the smallest bags of coal and slack Rosie had ever seen.

It was after six and night had long fallen when they finally got home. The room was freezing, icier than outside, with draughts sweeping through the window sash and under the door.

Expertly, Catherine lit the fire and soon it was blazing. "With the slack this should last for a couple of hours," she said. "Then we'll have to get into bed." She hung the kettle from a hook over the flames and, when it was boiled, watched in awe as Rosie poured the water over the tea bags in the mugs, gave a vigorous stir and the transparent liquid changed to tea. "Magic," she breathed.

Rosie was surprised at how good she found the bread and dripping. She was starving and thirsty, drinking cup after cup of tea. She felt warmer now in the candlelit room, with the fire making strange shadows on the high walls. Outside the lamps softened the streetscape and, gazing at the other houses, she wondered what kind of lives people led in all those dimly-lit rooms.

"Why are so many people going into that house?" She pointed across the way.

"That's Mr Graham's Dancing Academy," Catherine told her. "People learn all the latest steps there." She shivered. "But Mother says it's a tragic house. It used to belong to Mr Maginni who lived there with his wife and six children and started the dancing academy. Then his wife died from TB and every one of his children. Mother says Mr Maginni couldn't bear the place after that. He moved out and Mr Graham took over." They were silent then, until Catherine said, "We'd better move away from the window. When the Tans come, if they're drunk, they fire at everyone they see."

Rosie had drunk rather a lot of tea. Looking around the room she wondered, "Where's your toilet?"

"We don't have a toilet. There's a lavatory out in the back yard, but we don't use it."

"Don't be daft!" Rosie said, "You're not telling me you never use a toilet!"

"Of course I am."

People couldn't have been *that* different in 1920, Rosie thought. And she was bursting. She tried again, "What *do* you use then?"

"Those pos over there. She pointed at two discreet enamel shapes in the corner.

Oh no! Rosie closed her eyes. If she'd known about this she'd *definitely* have stayed in her own time!

Catherine was handing her one of them.

"I'm going to use the toilet out the back," she said firmly. "This . . . this . . . *thing* is horrible!"

The other girl was hurt. "I'm sorry you think so. We try to keep everything clean and – "

"I don't mean *that*! It's not your fault." Rosie was

instantly apologetic and in her rush to make amends did not think. "It's just that I'm used to a proper toilet and I thought everyone was."

Frowning at her, Catherine snapped, "Don't lie! People with proper toilets are posh, not dressed like you. But come on, you can use the lavatory out the back, since you're so high and mighty."

Taking a lighted candle, she set off brusquely, Rosie following. At the foot of the stairs they turned down the hall. Before they reached the back door, Rosie got the awful stench, ten times more powerful than any pong in the house.

Catherine stood outside, "Here, take the candle. I'm not going any farther. That stuff leaves a smell for days."

Rosie took a few steps, her runners squelching. Hastily she came back. "Why is it so bad?"

Catherine shrugged. "There's one lavatory for sixty people and it doesn't work. Everyone uses the pos and throws the slops out here."

Chastened, Rosie put privacy on hold.

The fire died down and the room was chilly. Catherine put out the candles except the one under the Sacred Heart picture. "He'll keep us safe," she said. In the flickering light, Rosie thought the exposed heart with its drops of blood and crown of thorns was more of a fright than a comfort. Well, at least his heart's in the right place this time, she mused.

Catherine undressed to her petticoat and socks and slipped under the bedclothes, using her jacket and dress as extra cover. Rosie followed suit. There was no sheet on the mattress which scratched where the stuffing came through. The pillow was a piece of rolled-up clothing. She thought of her electric blanket at home, her duvet, crisp cotton sheets and plump pillows.

The street lights went out. "Ten o'clock curfew," Catherine murmured. Rosie heard the scampering of tiny feet and tried to block them out. She could all too easily imagine rats running across her face. Instead, she concentrated on outside sounds. Hurrying footsteps on the pavement, the foghorn from the river. Then came a rumble in the distance and Catherine sat up. "It's the Tans' lorries – the Crossley tenders! Please don't let there be a raid tonight."

The sound came closer and they heard shouts and laughter and the smash of glass as a bottle hit the pavement.

"Don't let them be drunk!" Catherine was tense. But the lorries went on into the distance and she lay down again.

"Are the Tans really that bad?"

Catherine turned to her. "Can you remember nothing?"

"I remember food." Sharp pangs of hunger filled her with longing. All she had eaten today was a few slices of bread.

"What do you remember?"

Rosie hesitated, "You won't believe me."

"I don't care. Tell me something beautiful."

"I remember sizzling sausages and rashers. Chips. A Big Mac with lots of tomato ketchup – "

"Big what? How can a tomato catch up? You're codding me, Rosie. That's not nice."

"I amn't, I swear. It's minced beef with tomato sauce only much tastier. . . I remember sweet and sour chicken, vindaloo curry, spaghetti bolognese, corn on the cob, pizza, pasta, lasagne – "

"Wait a minute. Pizza, pasta, lasagne – that's not

food! You're just making up words. Tell me some real food."

Rosie thought hard. "Did you ever hear of ice cream? It's frozen cream with delicious flavours. I love it even in winter. It is *so* beautiful." She sighed, almost tasting.

"Go on. You can't stop now, Rosie."

"Mint or strawberry. Chocolate chip. Chocolate fudge. White chocolate." Getting carried away she chanted, "Viennetta, Magnum, Cornetto, Feast, Gino Ginelli, Tango Twist, Raspberry Ripple, Romantica . . . mmm."

"Lovely," Catherine breathed. "I don't care if you're making it up. Viennetta, Cornetto, Romantica," she rolled the words and Rosie was astonished at her memory. "Gino Ginelli and Tango Twist . . . I've never heard of anything so beautiful. But you've forgotten one flavour. You should have said peanut butter ice cream. That'd be the best. It's funny, but I'm not the least bit hungry any more."

Neither was Rosie. In fact, she was feeling slightly sick at her friend's last suggestion.

"I suppose peanut butter ice cream would be a bit better than fish-head ice cream," she said, but Catherine was breathing deeply, fast asleep.

Chapter 7

FOLEY WAS already there when they got to the Gresham next morning. William joined them in the recess. At a nod from Foley, he spoke first. "The guests are mostly families. Then there are a few foreigners and a few businessmen. Nothing out of the ordinary."

"Let me be the judge of that," Foley was quite sharp. "We'll start with the business types. Get a list of names for me from reception. Mr Callaghan will arrange it. And I'll want a detailed description of each man." He turned to the girls, "How did you get on?" They told him about McClean and his face lit up. "Well done!" he said. "Excellent!"

Rosie basked in his approval and, looking at his bright boyish face, lost some of her doubts.

Reading her mind, he said earnestly, "I swear to you, McClean is a bad man, responsible for ruining people's lives. He'd like to cheat my friends out of their money. By giving me this information you have saved a lot of people. I mean it, Rosie. Well done!" He smiled and she nodded, charmed at being singled out for his attention.

"With more comrades like you two," he said, "we could wipe out every villain in Ireland."

Newbury had used the same kind of words, Rosie remembered.

"Now, you said some arrangements were mentioned in the letter. Do you remember what they were?"

"Mclean is to be ready next week. That's what it said." Catherine told him.

Rosie was curious, "What does it all mean?"

"The less you know, the safer you'll be," Foley said. "I want you to go back to Morehampton Road. Not to McClean's, but to 110. A fellow called Clancy is staying there, waiting to hear from me. I don't want to put anything important in writing, but he will need proof that I sent you. Give him this." He pulled out a piece of paper and scribbled:

Urgent we proceed. Instructions with bearer. God Bless.

He did not sign the note. "Clancy knows my handwriting – now, has either of you got a good memory?"

Rosie, recalling how Catherine effortlessly repeated the list of Italian food, instantly pointed to her friend.

"Right, try this: 'McLean at number 117. Plans brought forward to Sunday. Nine bells will ring. Others may be at same address.'"

The little she understood of this made Rosie curious. "Are you looking for others as well as McLean?"

Foley nodded, "I learned yesterday there may be two more of the enemy in that house."

She looked at Catherine who shook her head. Neither of them mentioned the letters to Cadlow and Smith. Instead, Catherine repeated the message perfectly for Foley. He was pleased, then mused, "I wish we had a likeness of McLean and whoever else is staying in that house. Then we could be sure we're dealing with the right fellows."

Rosie grew red with excitement. The Polaroid camera! She could get Foley a picture!

She took a deep breath. "Remember you told us to ask no questions?" she said.

"Yes?"

"Well, if you ask no questions, I can get you a full colour photo of McClean and his friends."

Foley laughed, "A colour photograph! There's no such thing." Then as Rosie remained silent, his eyes sharpened, "How?"

"No questions," she smiled. "Otherwise no photograph."

He nodded slowly. "All right. I don't believe this, but there's nothing to lose."

"What are you up to?" Catherine asked as soon as they were alone.

"No questions," Rosie said sweetly and Catherine snapped, "I didn't make any promises and if you don't tell me what's going on, you can go over to Morehampton Road on your own. All that talk about photos! You have no camera, Rosie! You must be hallucinating. Even if you had one, McClean is hardly going to stand there smiling and posing while you set it on a tripod and put your head under a blanket to take his picture!" She sighed, frowning with worry. "Your brain must be getting worse instead of better."

Rosie's brain went into overtime. There was no point saying the camera came from the 1990s. Catherine would definitely think she belonged in an asylum. Instead she said, "You know that kit-bag I have? The army one? Well I found a camera in it, a small one, and according to the instructions it takes a photo instantly. And it develops that photo in less than a minute."

Catherine's face went through a range of expressions, from disbelief and sadness at her friend's obvious lunacy, to doubt, possible acceptance and then wonder. All the time her mouth opened and shut while she struggled to say something. At last she stopped swallowing and breathed, "It must be the latest British invention! A top secret military camera – "

"For spying," Rosie added helpfully.

"On the enemy," Catherine nodded, wide-eyed with awe. "Why they could photograph people, weapons, military manoeuvres without anybody realising . . . it's . . . it's . . . unbelievable." She focused sharply on her friend. "If this is true, Rosie, why didn't you tell me about it?"

"I forgot. Amnesia, remember!" She grinned. "You can see for yourself the minute we get back to the room."

"By the way," Rosie said a few moments later, "why didn't you want to tell Foley about those letters to Cadlow and Smith?"

"Because he would've been annoyed that we didn't open them. We can mention them after this visit – if they're still staying there."

It was their unspoken hope that Smith at least would somehow be gone. They had liked Tommy and, if his father was some sort of cheat, that was not his son's fault and they didn't want to cause him any grief.

By two o'clock in the afternoon they were in Donnybrook, Catherine still exclaiming every so often at the magical camera. She had been almost fearful when Rosie had taken her photo in front of the large tenement window. Watching the picture emerge, she had backed away. "It's working by itself," she breathed. "Nobody's touching it." As the photo began to form on the shiny paper she covered her eyes. "It's creepy," she whispered, "like a ghost appearing." She would not

79

touch it, shivering at her image. "You keep it!" she said and turned away.

Morehampton Road was busy. Horse traffic, a few motor-cars, trams and a Tan lorry, wheels screeching as usual. There were quite a few pedestrians, but no one they recognised. A middle-aged couple strolled along, walking their dog.

"Let's get behind them," Rosie said. "We'll be less noticeable."

Conscious of the figures close behind them, the couple quickened their pace. The two followed suit. A few more yards and they'd be at Clancy's. But, anxious to let them pass, the man and woman slowed down. So too did the girls.

The small spaniel thought this a wonderful game. He jumped up on Rosie, tail madly wagging. "Down, boy!" Rosie tried to push him away. The spaniel got hysterical with excitement and bounded at her, barking joyously. People turned to look. Desperate, Rosie hissed, "Will you get down!" and shoved him off.

He raced around in a narrow circle, his long silky ears flying wide, then returned to the attack, this time licking her hand, yapping at her to pat his head. She'd had enough. "Get off! Such a twit – mad animal – stop slobbering on me!"

Catherine was no help. Taking a fit of giggles, she was wiping her eyes and holding her side. Nor was the dog the only problem. Having ignored all the antics behind her up to this, now the woman stopped dead and Rosie fell over her, jerking the lead out of her hand.

"How dare you! How dare you insult my dog!"

Seated on the ground, Rosie couldn't answer. The spaniel was able to get at her more easily now that she was on the pavement. He was crooning happily, sitting on her lap and enthusiastically licking her face.

The woman was beside herself, "Panther! Stop licking this horrible urchin! Come away from her, Panther! Your paws will get filthy."

Panther! Catherine bent double with laughter. Scarlet, Rosie struggled with the spaniel. The irate woman ranted while her husband puffed mildly on his pipe, gazing into the distance. The number of spectators had grown.

Raging at her loss of dignity, Rosie hit the dog with her coat sleeve. At the same time his owner bent down to retrieve the lead and the spaniel bit her hand, convinced she had whacked him.

"Panther! Nasty, nasty doggie!" She made to smack him but he turned on her, snarling. Her husband took the pipe from his mouth, knocked it empty against the heel of his shoe and pocketed it. Then he lifted the dog and, clasping him under an arm, strode away. After a moment's hesitation the woman followed and the onlookers drifted off.

Rosie got to her feet and glared at her friend. "A great help you were!"

"'Panther! Stop it at once. Nasty, nasty Panther!'" Catherine was an excellent mimic and Rosie could only laugh.

Before they could turn into Clancy's they ran into Captain McClean, apparently also out for a stroll. Recognising them, he stopped. "Ah, the two young ladies who delivered my post yesterday. Not bringing more letters today?" He was joking, but Catherine got red and involuntarily clenched the note. Rosie shifted nervously, glad the camera was deep inside her pocket.

His smile disappeared and his eyes went from

Catherine's scarlet face to her closed fist. He said softly, "I can't believe we are so short of postmen. Let me see what you have there." Before they could move he had gripped Catherine's hand and tried to twist her fingers free of the paper. When she would not let go he wrenched her arm behind her back and Catherine gave a cry of pain. Prising the note from her hand he released her and stepped back, all the time staring at them, daring them to move.

It was not until he glanced down at Foley's words that Rosie shouted, "Run!" and took off.

Incensed at the way her arm had been twisted, Catherine managed to grab the note and kick McClean sharply on the ankle before following. The man shouted after them but they did not pause till they were well away. Then, doubled over in the effort to catch their breath, they leaned against a wall, recovering. At last Catherine said, "We have to see Clancy. Foley's message must be very important."

Fifteen minutes later, certain McClean was gone, they made their way back.

"We have a message for Mr Clancy," Catherine informed the man opening the door.

"'Tis myself you need, so." He must have been the same age as Foley, but his face was merry, on the verge of laughter, as if life were one big joke. Catherine handed him the grubby note and he was at once serious. "Reveal all," he said and Catherine recited: "Mr Foley says: 'McLean at number 117. Plans brought forward to Sunday. Nine bells will ring. Others may be at same address.'"

"How do you do that? That is *so* cool." Rosie was impressed.

So was Clancy. Smiling once more, he said,

"Excellent work. Tell Foley we'll be ready on Sunday." He closed the door abruptly. Taken aback, the girls had no choice but to turn on their heels.

Outside the gate Rosie stopped. "Now," she said, "you wait here. I'll go up to 117. If McClean is home I'll see if I can get his picture." Before Catherine could object, she was off.

She knocked, stepped back and taking the camera from her pocket quickly fixed the flash. Expecting the maid to appear, she held it behind her back. A man she had not seen before opened the door. She asked for Mr McClean. He looked amused and called, "Donald, there's someone here to see you."

"Who is it, Tom? Tell them I'm busy."

"It's a girl. Looks like an urchin." Already he was closing the door.

"Hold on to her. Don't let her go!" Footsteps came thundering downstairs. She could hear someone else rushing up the hall. Then the door was jerked wide open and there were three men in the entrance. They blinked in the dazzling flash.

"What's she doing? Tom! Cadlow! Get after her!"

Racing down the garden, Rosie wished she wasn't wearing a long dress. It flapped like a tent around her. With her free hand she lifted skirt and petticoat and ran for her life. The men rushed after her. Turning out the gate, Rosie caught a glimpse of Catherine's astonished face. Fit and athletic the three followed, one behind the other. Then McClean fell flat on his face, tripping over Catherine's outstretched foot and the other two stumbled, landing in a heap on top of him. Catherine ran. By the time McClean and his friends got to their feet, she and Rosie were well away.

Foley was waiting as he'd promised, arguing with

83

himself. He did not believe in colour photographs, but he did believe in Rosie. She's a plucky kid, he thought, yet there's something strange about her; the way she talks to me as an equal even though I'm much older. She isn't properly respectful and that's not like a normal kid. No matter what they do behind your back, I've never met one before who wasn't polite to your face. Telling me to do my own dirty work!

And she looks so healthy, tall and bright-eyed, not pasty faced and undersized like the usual tenement child. All right, she looks scruffy, but she's not too comfortable in those clothes she wears. She doesn't belong here. She doesn't blend in like Catherine and William . . . and the words she uses . . . maybe she *can* get a colour picture of McClean . . .

No one wanted to get the wrong men. Professional pride was at stake here – and a lot more. There would be no sympathy if the innocent suffered. Besides, the apostles had never botched up a job yet. The British were very close to getting their hands on Collins's secret bank-books. According to sources it would take their agents less than a week to crack the coded information they'd got from their informers. Then they'd swoop on the banks and seize everything. It was up to the apostles to stop them. Michael Collins would be very upset if his band of twelve did not perform well. He had picked them for their youth and bravery, for their dedication. He trusted them completely. They could not let him down . . .

"Here it is!" A hurricane burst into the alcove off the Gresham's kitchens.

"Rosie was nearly caught!"

"Yes, but Catherine tripped them up!"

The girls were gasping with excitement. They had

run from the Pillar terminus in their haste to present their trophy and now they were out of breath, waving the photo at him. Foley grabbed it, looked, and could scarcely believe his eyes.

"You did it! You did it!" He whooped. "You're geniuses!" Jumping up, he seized both of them by the arm and whirled them around in a jig of joy.

"Mind the photo!" Rosie twisted out of his grasp. But there was no stopping Foley's happiness. He took off his hat and flung it high, and when it fell he tap-danced around it on the floor, singing 'It's a long way to Tipperary' faster than they'd ever heard it before, matching it to the mad gallop he was doing around the hat.

"That's lovely, that is. The dance of the demented lunatic!" Rosie was sarcastic, trying to hide her pleasure at his reaction. The other two were grinning away and she had to laugh with them. Foley was like a schoolboy who'd been given his summer holidays. Ecstatic. He no longer looked threatening or sinister.

Seated again, he studied the picture. "This one is McClean," he pointed accurately. "And these are the other boyos, Cadlow and Thomas Herbert Smith! Excellent."

At that moment William came into the alcove. "Mister Callaghan says to please keep the noise down. The manager will be on his rounds soon and if he finds you, there'll be trouble."

"Have a look at this, William," Foley passed the photo. "Have you ever seen anything like it? A pity Rosie won't tell us about her camera – "

"I know him," William interrupted. "That man there!" He was pointing at Smith.

Foley was all attention, the jovial smile disappearing. "Smith? How do you know him?"

"I saw him talking to two of the guests in the bar this morning, just after you left, Mr Foley. They were in a corner booth and kept looking around to see if anyone was watching. They didn't pay any attention to me, though, and that fellow, Smith, left soon after in a motor-car."

"That's the beauty of using people like you to spy, William. You're invisible."

"Thanks very much!" The boy was huffy. "If you're saying people never notice me – "

"No offence," Foley said. "It's like you said yourself. They paid no attention to you. That's because you're staff, in uniform. They'd never have dreamed you could be spying on them. Would you recognise Smith's companions again?"

"Oh, I can do better than that!" William was positively smug. "I pointed them out to Mister Callaghan later in the dining-room. They were at different tables and didn't even look at each other. Mr Callaghan found out that one of them is staying in room 24. A Mr McCormack. The other man's name is Mr Wilde and he's in number 14 . . ."

In his excitement Foley leapt from his chair and whacked William on the arm. The alcove could scarcely contain him now. "We have them!" He was exultant. "We have the enemy! Imagine, McClean, Smith and Cadlow in Morehampton Road. Wilde and McCormack here. Ah this is a great day!" He began to pace up and down. "Villains, all of them," he said, "sly and treacherous. Scum of the earth!"

He registered the astonished faces of the others and stopped his tirade at once, breathing deeply until he was calm again. "Believe me," he went on, "they are all cheats. Clancy and I had to track those five. They are part of a much wider network of villains, all of whose whereabouts are now known. Soon we will bring them to justice."

Rosie was relieved to hear the word "justice". Foley had been spitting venom and for a moment she'd been afraid for the men they'd spied on. But if they were arrested and brought to trial, there was little chance of them going to prison, if they were innocent. She hoped Captain McClean was innocent. There was something nice about him when he'd read that letter, just as there was about Foley when he'd danced madly around his hat only moments before. Of course McLean had been horrible to Catherine. But then Foley had looked positively vicious when he'd spoken about "the enemy."

Flushed with success, Foley grinned at them, "Tomorrow," he said, "you're having a day off – with pay and expenses." From a pocketful of money he extracted three half-crowns. Catherine and William kept thanking him.

Thirty old pennies – that's about 13p, Rosie thought. She could not get hyper about 13p, like the other two. They're nearly hysterical, she mused, scornfully. Then, remembering the cold, bare tenement room she felt ashamed.

"Go to the picture-house. Buy some sweets," Foley was telling them, "and come back here on Thursday."

"I'll get some flowers for mother," Catherine said, "and a box of chocolates. We'll bring them up to the hospital tomorrow night."

As they were leaving, Foley was still praising them. "Your help has been useful, though even without it we'd have caught McClean and his friends." His eyes chilled.

"Now they'll pay for their crimes." His words were low and they strained to hear, "The hunters are closing in . . ." And Rosie, cold with fear, was never afterwards sure whether it was her imagination or Foley that added, "closing in for the kill."

They were quiet on the way home, Rosie brooding on the events of the day, hoping life would become less complicated as the week wore on.

Catherine's train of thought was evident when she said, "Will you come with me tomorrow night when I visit Mother? She'd like to meet you." Rosie nodded and Catherine went on, "I hope she's better. She was so tired after the flu and she worries about Father. She thinks something must have happened to him." Her face was strained and Rosie tried to imagine how she would feel if Mom were ill and Dad missing.

Catherine spent a chunk of their money on the party, buying cooked meats in Findlater's and loaves of fresh bread in Kennedy's. Rosie sighed but decided it was useless to object.

They were almost home, making their way along Great Denmark Street, when they heard a slow rumble.

"Tans!" Catherine's voice was terse. "They're going to stop. Quick. Hide!" The few pedestrians evaporated, suddenly turning into shops or alleyways. But further down the road two small girls continued skipping, oblivious to the danger.

"Over here!" Catherine dived down some basement steps, Rosie following.

"*Please*, don't stop!" Catherine's eyes closed briefly, then peering through the railings she called to the small girls, "Get off the street! Go in!" But they didn't hear, absorbed in their game.

Now the lorries had turned the corner, moving

slowly. "They're looking for someone," Catherine whispered. High above them a shot rang out, the bullet ricocheting on the pavement near the first lorry. Engines were left running and they heard the cab doors open and slam and the clatter of boots and rifles as the soldiers piled from the covered convoy.

What was happening? Petrified but dying of curiosity, Rosie raised her head a fraction. The soldiers were hiding behind the lorries which were less than six feet away. Then, from around the rear wheels of the first one, a face peered. Catching sight of Rosie, the man raised his rifle. Frozen with terror, she could not move.

Afterwards she remembered every detail as if it had happened in slow motion. Etched in her mind was the soldier's young face, his dark cap, the glint of the barrel in the weak afternoon sunlight. His mouth was slightly open, his dark eyes afraid.

Having raised his gun he too became frozen, both of them caught in mutual terror. The silence was broken by a volley from the front of the lorry. Two soldiers were firing at a window somewhere above their heads. There was no answering shot.

"Can you see anybody?" one of them yelled at his companions.

"There's no one out there, sir!" came the reply. "The sniper's gone and the street is empty." Rosie's soldier remained silent, never taking his eyes off her.

"Quick. Back in the lorries!" Instantly they piled in, the young man seated at the back, still staring at her, his rifle across his knees, no longer a threat. She thought she saw him smile and, as the lorries took off, he definitely raised his hand in a salute.

Beside her, Catherine relaxed, "I hate it when they

stop. Sometimes, when they can't find who they want, they pick on anyone."

"I think they were just as terrified as us," Rosie reflected.

"It doesn't matter," Catherine shrugged, "they still kill."

Up the street a hysterical mother was berating the two little girls. "Why don't you ever listen? What did I tell you? What are you supposed to do when you see the Tans?" Each question was followed by a clip on the ear. "Answer me. What did I tell you to do?" She was shaking them now and they had begun to wail.

"You told us to come in immediately," one of them sobbed.

"And did you? Did you? No! You did not! Do you not remember what happened to poor Annie O'Neill on Saturday?" Now the mother was sobbing herself and hugging the two weeping children. Neighbours arrived to comfort her and add their word of warning:

"You must do what your mother says."

"You have to run in the minute you see the Tans."

"You don't want to end up like poor Annie O'Neill!"

"Who was Annie O'Neill?" Rosie asked as they moved away. "What on earth happened to her?"

"She was killed on Saturday by the Tans." Catherine was sombre. "Same age as us. Shot in the heart when she was outside her house in Charlemont Street talking to friends."

Fear struck Rosie afresh. Surely nobody waged war against twelve-year-olds . . .

"Did they kill her deliberately?"

"I suppose not. They were after some men who were playing pitch-and-toss at the corner. When the Tans came the men scattered and shots were fired. Annie

O'Neill was killed and another little one was hit in the arm."

"So it was an accident?" Rosie felt some relief.

"Probably." Catherine was silent for a second, then burst out, "But they'd sicken you. The Auxie officer said only one shot was fired. How could one shot hit two people like that? They *never* tell the truth and they *never* have to answer for what they do!"

Chapter 8

THE TENEMENT was buzzing. Everyone was looking forward to the hooley.

Mrs Hennessey was delighted with their purchases. "This'll be the best night we've had in ages. Mr H and the boys are gone off to fetch jugs of porter. The neighbours have been bringing bits and pieces all day, even lumps of coal. Maybe you'd give Lilian and me a hand getting the place ready."

At that moment her daughter staggered in the door carrying a large contraption with a trumpet attached. "Mr Dempsey's gramophone weighs a ton," she gasped, setting it down on the sofa which groaned and creaked from the strain.

"Are you better, Lilian?" Catherine asked.

"Convalescing," Mrs H said quickly as her daughter glared, adding, "Now, Lilian, if you want to go to Croke Park on Sunday with your friends you have to be completely well."

"Oh, she'd be better off not going to Croke Park at all," Rosie blurted.

Lilian's eyes narrowed in rage. "Interfering busybody!" she seethed.

"That's enough, Miss! Rosie's only thinking of you.

You're not fully better yet, for all you say. You could catch your death at that match."

Rosie shuddered at the words. Suppose her grandmother *did* go to Croke Park? Suppose she got killed?"

"But you *promised* I could go with Catherine and William. Everyone will be there. You're letting the boys go with Father! You can't go back on your word to me. It's terrible staying in all day with nothing to do. And I am better . . . you said . . ."

Lilian stopped, near to tears. Mrs Hennessey was soothing, "Of course you'll go. Nobody wants you to be a coffin case, that's all. But if you stay in for the rest of the week, you're bound to be better. Now, let's get everything sorted out for tonight."

By eight o'clock the tenement room was crowded with cheerful neighbours; men and women sipping porter and whiskey, children staring at the packed table, not yet allowed to eat. The fire was blazing, almost too hot. An old oil lamp and some candles provided soft light.

"A king's feast," Mrs Henderson had said earlier when they'd finished stacking the table with sandwiches, broken the chocolate into a dish and filled the pot noodles far too early with hot water. "Nobody'll care if it goes cold," Mrs H assured Rosie, "Sure they'd eat it dry." The beans were cold too. Rosie was certain no one in their right minds would touch them.

The neighbours brought various offerings. Tripe was a favourite. One look at the pieces of sheeps' stomach floating in a thick gluey liquid made her feel sick and she was unable to investigate further. There was probably even a fish-head stew hovering in one of the lidded pots.

Her great-uncles arrived just before the party began in earnest. Carrying in jugs of porter with such intense concentration, they gave an impression of serious character which was quite misleading. As soon as they'd set down the liquid, a wrestling match started which might have toppled the contents of the table. However, the tall man behind them roared, "Joseph! Jamesie! Christy! Stop your foolishness at once or I'll larrup you!" He grabbed the smallest by the scruff of the neck and held him in the air till he ceased kicking. The other two rolled out of range, stood up and giggled.

Order was restored and the tall bearded man grinned at Rosie. "You must be the child the missus keeps talking about," he said, "the one who robbed the British army! Put it there." He held out a hand and shook hers vigorously. "A daring deed," he said, "And it's a pity you can't remember how you went about it, for we could all do with some lessons."

William was the last to arrive, just after eight. Unnoticed by Rosie some signal was given. Stews, tripe and coddle disappeared along with the chocolate and curry, so fast Rosie thought they must have been eaten together.

The crowd was like a giant hoover. They converged upon the table, blocking it from view and when they left it again a few minutes later, everything was gone.

Rosie was introduced to the neighbours as the heroine of the hour. "Robbed the British army, so she did," her great-grandfather told everyone. "How she swiped a kit-bag from under their noses I do not know. Of course, neither does she!"

He paused, giving people time to murmur their wonder and appreciation. "The poor child remembers nothing. Suffering from insomnia, so she is." The neighbours looked at her with grave concern and Rosie giggled.

"I don't have insomnia," she assured them.

"Of course you have. You remember nothing." Her great-grandfather was adamant. Rosie decided he was a little tipsy. Now the neighbours were murmuring condolences.

"Is it not *amnesia* I have?" People seemed to have a problem with the word and she did not like to contradict him outright.

"Of course it is." He patted her shoulder, nodding at the neighbours, "What did I tell you? The poor kid can't even remember what's wrong with her."

Later on the dancing started. Furniture was pushed to one side. Mr Dempsey's gramophone was wound up, a Strauss waltz began and assorted couples took to the floor. The women were determined to have a go. They danced with their men folk, they danced with each other, they danced with small girls and very reluctant small boys. Rosie was swept up by an ample lady whose grip was unrelenting and who sighed when Rosie stumbled, grasping her even tighter and lifting her off the floor. She felt like a big parcel. When the waltz was over the woman said kindly, "You did your best, love, but you need a few lessons. You dance like a flamin' horse. Would you like me to teach you?"

Rosie was indignant. "I do not dance like a flamin' horse. In fact, I'm the best in my class at rave."

"Rave? Never heard of it. Is it the latest? Let me see how it's done, love."

She would not take "no" for an answer. "'God Save Ireland' said the heroes," was next on the gramophone. It was unlike any rave music Rosie had ever heard. Nevertheless, she did her best, arms and legs gyrating

95

awkwardly in the effort to match the marching rhythm.

The ample lady was nodding her head sagely. "I can see why you call it 'rave' love. It's because you look like a ravin' lunatic, isn't it? Never mind, I'm sure they'll find a cure for you one day." She smiled sympathetically and turned away in search of a better partner.

Next came the set dances and the floorboards strained under the jigs and reels. People flung themselves into the "Siege of Ennis" as if they were on a real attack. William and Catherine missed the wall by a few inches. Afterwards, exhausted, Catherine slumped down beside Lilian on the sofa and William made his way over to Rosie.

"What was that dance you were doing earlier?" he asked.

Rosie groaned inwardly. "Rave," she said.

"It looked very interesting. Would you show me how to do it?"

Rosie looked at him sharply, but he was deadly serious. "You haven't got the right music," she said, "It has to be different, faster for a start."

"That's no problem. I'll put on 'Sweet Marie'."

Oh God, Rosie thought when she heard the song. William stood in front of her, eagerly waiting. Once again she did her best. Listening to the chorus, she wondered what kind of a girl sweet Marie was. She seemed to keep running away from her boyfriend. Maybe it was because he fell on every daisy he met. Were all the old songs as strange? she wondered.

"Hould your holt, sweet Marie,
If you bolt, sweet Marie,
Sure you'll never get across the field for me.

All the daisies in the dell Ought to know me mighty
well,
For on every one I fell, sweet Marie."

William was entranced. "This is the berries. You
don't have to learn any steps."

A number of people joined in, enthusiastically
waving their arms and legs around. To Rosie they
looked comical. Then she heard the ample lady say very
loudly, "Isn't it well William picked a song about a horse
for that young one."

"Don't mind her," William whispered. "Two-ton-
Tessie!"

Rosie giggled.

"Do you find everything is very strange here?" The
boy asked.

She stared at him. What was he getting at? He
couldn't possibly know . . .

"It must be awful," he went on, "not remembering
what happened last week or last year."

Rosie mumbled a reply. He was so sympathetic she
felt ashamed of her deception. He went on, "Maybe if
we look at the clues we might get nearer to finding out
about you. First of all you have a Dublin accent, even if
it's a bit posher than mine. But your clothes are like
Catherine's, so that means you're not well off. You're
not from this area either, otherwise people would know
you. And when Catherine met you outside the house
you weren't feeling well. So you wouldn't have had the
strength to travel far. You must live somewhere in
town."

He paused, his eyes narrowed in concentration.

"What you need is something to jog your memory."
His face brightened. "I've got a half-day tomorrow. The
three of us could have a look round the city. That way

someone might recognise you, or you might see some place you remember. It's worth a try."

Rosie tried to match his enthusiasm. It was kind of him to be concerned. He was good fun, she thought. An afternoon exploring the city with him and Catherine would be an adventure, even though there was no hope of his mission succeeding.

"I'd like to go up Nelson's Pillar," she said.

William was startled. "I don't think you lived up there," he grinned.

"No, but you can see a lot of the city from there. I might recognise something."

"Great idea! Why didn't I think of that?" His admiration was so obvious she liked him even more.

Then across the room she caught Lilian staring at her. Catherine was not with her and in the midst of the crowd she looked lonely. Rosie went over.

"Why did you say anything to Mother about Croke Park?" Lilian attacked her immediately. "I've been looking forward to it for weeks."

Rosie hesitated, then made her decision. "Because people will get killed at that match," she said quietly.

"Oh, and did you tell this to Catherine? No, I can see you didn't! When did anyone ever get killed at a football match? You're just jealous of me being friends with Catherine and you don't want me to go anywhere with her. She's my best friend and you're not going to change anything, no matter how much you lie."

"But I don't want to change anything." Rosie was stunned. How could her grandmother of all people believe such horrible things? Lilian wasn't finished, "You think you're the berries, making everyone believe you're so brave and having them feel sorry because you

98

can't remember a thing. But you didn't lose your memory, did you?"

Even in the candlelight she could see Rosie's face blaze. Triumphantly she smiled. "I knew it! You are so *sly*!"

Stung at last into a response – after all this was the person she'd come back to help – Rosie snapped, "You've got it all wrong. It's you who's jealous of me because you're stuck in all the time and – "

"A bit of hush, *please*!" Her great-grandfather announced. "Mrs O'Brien will now sing for us her favourite melody 'I dreamt I dwelt in marble halls.'" Whistles and claps followed, then everyone was silent as she began. Her face was twisted in agony and her hands clasped prayerfully as she sang. Rosie wondered if she were in pain. Apparently not; she sang beautifully and finished to loud applause.

Then a young man sang "Nora" in a clear haunting voice and after him each of the neighbours took a turn. Rosie was amazed at how well they sang and how sad the songs were. The more heart-wrenching lyrics got the loudest applause.

After "She is far from the land," the atmosphere was sombre and the young man with the haunting voice stepped forward again, speaking shyly. "I heard a new song on a street corner only yesterday. The lad was kind enough to give me the words. It's in remembrance of Kevin Barry, executed exactly fifteen days ago."

The room was silent as he sang.

"In Mountjoy jail one Monday morning,
High upon the gallows tree
Kevin Barry gave his young life
For the cause of liberty.

99

Just a lad of eighteen summers
Now there's no one can deny
As he walked to death that morning
He proudly held his head on high."

The song was familiar to Rosie and it had always given
her a pain because it was so dreary. Now the young
man's sincerity, his sweet soaring voice and the
reverence in the room all created a poignant melody.
When he was finished there was no applause, only
silence.

Then Mr H cleared his throat and said, "We must
have one last song to finish the night, and who better to
sing than our new friend Rosie!"

Dismayed, Rosie found herself pushed forward. No
one else had refused. She could plead loss of memory. It
wasn't as if she had a good voice. Miss Graham once
told her she'd never have to worry about unemployment
when she grew up: she'd always get a job as a foghorn.
And Mom hadn't been much better. She'd banged on
the bathroom door when Rosie was singing her
favourite number and roared at her to stop trumpeting
like an elephant.

But suddenly she decided the party could do with a
lift and, crossing her fingers for luck, she threw herself
into "Park Life" by blur.

"Know what I mean.
I get up when I want
Except on Wednesdays
When I get rudely awakened by the dustman.
Park life.
I put my trousers on,
And I think about leaving the house.

Park life
I feed the pigeons.
I sometimes feed the sparrows too.
It gives me an enormous sense of wellbeing.
Park life."

blur would not have recognised the melody.

This time the atmosphere was not so much respectful as shocked.

"It'd be just as well if that young one lost her memory again," Mrs O'Brien said.

"Does she have chronic asthma? Is it her bronchials?" a man enquired.

"She as good as told me she was ravin'!" Her dancing partner, the ample lady, informed them.

"Nobody should have to suffer like that," Mr Dempsey said.

"Ah sure, God help the poor young one!"

"I wasn't talking about *her* suffering!" Mr Dempsey snapped, "It's us who need protection. She's like a thousand frogs croaking at once!"

It probably had nothing to do with her singing, but the party broke up soon afterwards.

"That was a great night," Catherine said as they got ready for sleep, then added mischievously, "in spite of your voice." Rosie would have thrown a pillow at her if she'd had one.

They discussed William's plans for the next afternoon. "He's very nice, isn't he?" Rosie said, thinking of his concern.

"William? He's the best!"

In the darkness Rosie began to think of Lilian. The insults still rankled. Although she'd been attacked and called a liar, she had caught a flash of fear in her grandmother's eyes when she'd warned her about Sunday.

Brooding on the hostility between them, something occurred to her at last. "How could I be so thick as not to see it before? I'm that girl Gran didn't like, whose name she couldn't remember . . . she says I can't change anything, but this time I don't want to. All I want to do is find out what happens to Catherine next Sunday." She pondered, "What if Gran does go to the match? Something horrible could happen. She could even be killed. And what would that mean for Mom and me? This time things *have* to stay the same."

Chapter 9

"WHAT'S YOUR school like?" Rosie asked Catherine over breakfast the next morning.

For some reason she'd been thinking about Miss Graham and how cross she was. Then she remembered Miss Hackett from the fifties. Miss Hackett had been truly horrible.

Do teachers have to pass an exam in grumpiness before they're allowed into the classroom? she wondered. Even Stormin' Norman, who'd taught her in fifth class and whom she'd liked because he was fair — even he wouldn't have won an award for cheerfulness. Definitely not a laugh a minute. Maybe teachers were born grumpy. For a second she imagined a baby Miss Graham making cross imperious noises from her pram.

"I love school," Catherine said.

Rosie had never met anyone before who'd admitted even to liking school, never mind loving it. Astonished, she stared at her friend. "What's so great about it?"

"I love when I get sums right," Catherine said. "And I love having a fresh slate because the chalk writing always looks so white and new. It's great when it's my turn to read. Miss Gummer did *Jane Eyre* with us. That's the most beautiful book in the world. And I love it when she asks me to make the ink and I get it a really nice blue with just the right mixture of powder and water. Writing on paper is the best though. When she gives us a perfectly clean sheet and I don't get a blot on it and all my letters are clear and straight. That's the berries!"

Remembering Catherine's mention of Miss Gummer in her letters to Gran, Rosie could hardly believe her ears

"Are you sure you like Miss Gummer?"

"Of course I do. I just wish she'd stop giving me sewing to do. She thinks I'm not interested in school any more because I've missed so much time. She does get cross, but that's because she has to teach three classes at the one time. It's not easy, she says, to manage nearly sixty pupils."

"Does she hit you?" Rosie was remembering Miss Hackett and her bamboo cane.

"She does. If you talk, or if you don't understand her, or if you daydream she slaps you once on the hand with her leather strap. I think she only does it because she's supposed to. Afterwards, she's always very nice to the person she slapped. Not like Miss O'Malley." Catherine paused and her mouth tightened.

What about her?" Rosie prompted.

"She teaches the seven-year-olds and she has a thick heavy ruler." Catherine's eyes were bleak. "She uses the side of it and sometimes it cuts people's hands. The least she ever gives is six slaps. Mary O'Grady had to go into hospital after the beating she got."

Rosie was shocked. "How could that happen?"

"Because Miss O'Malley is so horrible. Mary doesn't have boots or socks and her feet and legs were scabby with sores from the cold. She couldn't do her writing.

Probably her hands were freezing and she couldn't hold the pen properly. Her page was full of blots. Miss O'Malley was raging at the mess. She said Mary did it deliberately and made her stand up on the table and pull her skirt up to her knees. Then she got the ruler and beat her legs with the side of it. She had to grab Mary's dress to keep her still. All the time the little one was crying and begging her to stop but she wouldn't, not until Mary's legs were like pulp and she fainted. She only stopped then because she couldn't keep her steady any more."

"That's vicious! She must be rotten!" Rosie was seething. "Was she arrested? She should have been tied into a straitjacket and put away forever!"

Rosie could not believe such cruelty. At least in the nineties teachers only assaulted your eardrums with the odd roar.

"Sure no one would arrest a teacher!" Catherine was scathing. "They're always right. Sister Benvenuta, the head nun, said Mary was very bold and shouldn't have aggravated Miss O'Malley."

"What about her parents? Did they do nothing?"

"Her mother has six others to look after and her father died last year. After she came out of hospital Mary went back to school and nothing was ever said. I'm glad Miss O'Malley's not my teacher."

For a while they were silent, mulling over the suffering of the little girl.

The cold comfortless room increased their gloom and some time later Rosie suggested a walk to pass the time before William came. It was a bright crisp morning. Lost in thought the girls meandered with no particular destination in mind.

Rosie was startled out of her wits. There was a

thunderous sound of hooves. Looking up, she clutched Catherine. "What's happening?" Thousands of cattle were pounding along the road towards her. "Oh, my God! We'll be killed. It's a stampede!"

"No, it's not – it's Wednesday!" Catherine laughed.

The logic of this escaped Rosie. Her friend tried again. "The Wednesday cattle drive, Rosie! From the North Circular Road, where we are now, to the North Wall. Remember?"

By this time the cows had slowed down, brought under control by men with switches. She held her breath as they ambled by, some of them stopping to drink at the troughs. A suburban child, Rosie had never before seen a cow on the streets of Dublin. They belonged in fields. Far away. Now one of them was eyeing her fondly and Rosie wanted nothing to do with it. The animal made its way determinedly up to her.

"Oooh, no-o-o . . ." She wailed and gripped Catherine tighter. The cow nudged her, then began to chew the sleeve of her coat. Her arm would be next! The scream stuck in her throat.

Catherine tried to free herself. "Lemme go. You're giving me pins and needles." She pushed Rosie, dislodging the beast, who snorted reproachfully and took after its companions.

"Imagine being afraid of a cow!" Catherine was scornful.

"It was eating me!" Rosie protested. Her friend began to giggle. After a moment, Rosie saw the funny side too and began to laugh. They became hysterical with mirth.

Feeling much better, they turned towards home to wait for William.

"Let's climb Nelson's Pillar first," Rosie said. She was thrilled at the prospect. It would be fun to go up the famous monument which no longer existed in her own time. Older people still talked about it and missed it, especially if they were like Mom and had never taken the opportunity to climb it.

"Righteo!" William led the way across Sackville Street. He had changed out of his uniform jacket into an overcoat and wore it like Foley wore his – open and swinging loose. It gave him a dashing air, especially with his workman's cap tipped to one side.

Inside the entrance at the base was a small booth where the ticket attendant took their money and waved them towards the spiral staircase with the warning: "The following are prohibited: All pushing and shoving. Chasing and other such shenanigans. The disposal of rubbish. The writing of names or other marks on his lordship's pedestal. Ascending the railing with the intention of jumping off, thereby causing a public nuisance and endangering the populace."

William was fascinated. "Did you make that up yourself?" he asked.

The attendant grinned. "Some of it. It's how I pass the time waiting for people to visit."

Rosie felt dizzy after climbing the long narrow spiral staircase. Her head was spinning and for some moments she closed her eyes and gripped the railing which edged the square platform at the base of the statue. When she finally looked down her head spun again. They were so high up!

Everything below looked small and distant, even the trams, while people farther away were tiny. She glanced at the GPO and caught her breath. The roof was gone. Only blackened crossbeams remained in place. The inside was gutted, only the charred walls left. What must it have been like to be inside when the shells were falling?

Looking down on the city's roofs, she was surprised to see so many tall chimney stacks sending trails of smoke across the November sky. Lazily they drifted in the breeze towards the Liffey, disappearing into the distance. She thought of cosy rooms and log fires and suddenly she was lonely for home and Sunday afternoons when the hearth blazed and everything was right with the world.

"Do you see any place you recognise?" William asked.

"Only Clery's and the river and the bridge," she said truthfully.

He looked disappointed, then his face brightened. "Maybe we should go down the quays. You might live somewhere off the river."

"Which way?" he said, when they reached the bridge. She waved a hand towards the Custom House. It was as good a direction as any.

Now, as she stood on the quayside, she was fascinated. Such a lot of activity. So many horses and carts, so much loading and unloading of cargo on and off old-fashioned ships. Barrels of Guinness were unloaded from barges. Wooden boxes were lifted off boats from England. A ferry was taking passengers across to the south quays. The port was lined with ships from all over the world. Some of them had exotic names. One fat old tub, she noticed, was called *The Empress of India*.

The quayside was dotted with small knots of men, always grouped around a more authoritative figure. Sometimes they were pleading, sometimes arguing. Such a group was near her and she moved closer to listen.

"Come on, Mr Gallagher, there's a ship just in. I've

had no work for the past week and no food for the table."

"I've done you proud, Mr G. No gaffer could have a better man! Give us a couple of hours loading."

"You promised me, Mr Gallagher. I've rent to pay. If I don't find work, we're evicted."

The figure in authority looked weary. "I'd have work for all of you if I could, but we've filled our quota. The boats have enough dockers now. Try again tomorrow."

The men turned away, cap in hand, trudging on to the next group.

The noise in the port was tremendous: neighing horses, wheels rattling on the cobblestones, shunting cargo, the shouts of men. Rosie could not ever remember such activity in the nineties.

She noticed something else too. As work began on unloading a coal ship, hordes of children came out of nowhere. Barefoot, they gathered around the cargo as it was stacked on to the quay, their backs bent, picking and rooting like small animals. "It's the coal," she realised at last. "They're collecting whatever falls out of the the sacks!"

Black and grimy, covered in coal dust, they looked as if they'd emerged from under the ground. Swiftly they filled old pots and bowls or ancient shopping bags. A couple of girls were piling the stuff into their aprons, pausing only to wipe their runny noses on filthy sleeves.

None of them was deterred by the coal hauliers' efforts to scatter them. Rosie saw one boy get a blow to the back of the head that knocked him over. Picking himself up, he moved a few yards away and continued his task as if nothing had happened. When there was no more to scavenge they melted away, clutching their hauls tightly.

Rosie had never seen so many barefoot children. She wondered if there were people as poor as these in the nineties. Another thought occurred. "If I'd lived then, I'd have been poor too." Maybe her friends could say the same. How many of their grandparents had lived through such bad times?

Suddenly she was sick of pretending, of letting William think he could find her home.

Yet she could not tell him the truth. "Why should you care where I live?" she burst out. "Why should it matter to you that I've lost my memory?"

"He's only trying to help!" Catherine was furious.

"I know what it's like, Rosie, to have no parents." His voice was gentle. "I didn't mean to interfere. It's just . . . well, if I thought there was a family somewhere that belonged to me, I couldn't bear not to find them. It must be lonely knowing they might be near, yet not be able to reach them."

"It is." Rosie sighed, twice as ashamed of herself now. "I'm sorry, William. I know you're trying to help, but I get tired thinking about it. It's no good. I can't see a way to get home just now."

Catherine was at once sympathetic. "Sometimes, the more you worry about a problem the harder it is to solve. Let's forget about where you come from for today."

Rosie was grateful. She could not hide her relief and William looked at her curiously. Before he could say anything a voice called him from the river. "William! Is that young William Scott?"

A man was standing on the quayside beside a Guinness barge.

"Matt Flanagan!" William strode over, the girls following.

"Matt used to deliver the porter to the hotel," he told them by way of introduction. "Now he works on the barges." The man nodded shyly at them, his smile gap-toothed.

"Would yourself and your lady friends like a wee trip up the Liffey? I'm taking her back to be reloaded."

Eagerly they nodded and he helped the girls aboard. They sat up near the engine house. Matt opened a small furnace and threw in a few shovels of coal. Then he fiddled with some gauges. "Ready to go!" He shouted at William who was still standing on the quay. Immediately the boy untied the rope from a small pillar and jumped into the barge. The man pulled a lever. There was a hiss of steam and smoke belched from a funnel over the engine house. They were off. Matt gripped the wheel and steered their course upriver.

In the gathering dusk Rosie saw the lights of other boats. All along the docks the streetlamps were lit. The black water danced with gold and orange reflections. Rosie noticed a strange edifice on the quayside. It was made of wrought iron, shaped like a small domed temple. Glinting yellow in the lamplight, it looked beautiful. The slow progress of the barge made it possible for her to notice a succession of men going in and coming out a few minutes later.

"Is that a little church?" She pointed to the structure. "Are those men going in to pray?"

Catherine was too startled to reply and William took a fit of laughing.

"It's a gents' lavatory," Catherine said at last when she saw Rosie wasn't joking.

"They're definitely not going in to pray!" William gasped between fits of giggles. This witticism made him laugh even more and he was doubled up, wiping his eyes and clutching his side.

Rosie was amazed. Imagine making beautiful public toilets when people had none in their homes!

How magical the city was in this light. The barge floated under the Ha'penny Bridge, past the Four Courts and on towards St James's Gate. All along the river were junk shops and second-hand bookshops, their treasures set up on stalls outside to attract the passer-by. Soon the silhouette of Kingsbridge Station loomed against the darkening sky. Twice Matt sounded the hooter and the three of them jumped with fright. He steered the boat towards the quayside. Where a man was waiting to tie her up. Barrels of porter were lined up, ready to be loaded.

"Thank you very much. That was the best boat trip I've ever had!" Rosie put out her hand and Matt shook it, beaming at her.

"That was the best laugh I ever had," William told her as they made their way home. By the time they reached the Gresham the Angelus bells were ringing. "Six o'clock!" Catherine groaned. "We'll have to run, Rosie. We've to go to the hospital in another hour. See you tomorrow, William, when we call on Foley."

Chapter 10

"I WANT YOU to bring these to the hospital. It's a few scones I baked on the griddle this afternoon." Mrs Hennessey was the latest neighbour to arrive at the room with a gift for Catherine's mother. So far she had received a packet of dates, two apples, a bag of sweets and a couple of slices of spiced beef.

"Be sure to tell Mrs Dalton we're all asking for her – and that we're trying to keep an eye on you – only you're never in. What are you up to at all?"

"We got a job, Mrs Hennessey, doing messages for someone . . ." Catherine was deliberately vague. Mrs Hennessey wasn't. "What someone would that be, exactly?" Rosie thought her great-grandmother very nosy. In her own time a neighbour would never ask such questions.

"A man in the Gresham hired us," Catherine said. "You don't have to worry, Mrs H. He's very nice to us."

"Well, I hope so! And I hope he's paying you properly! At least a shilling a day."

"Oh, a half-a – " Rosie didn't get to finish.

" – A half a day's work is what we usually do for him," Catherine rushed in, "And he pays well."

Mrs Hennessey went off satisfied. Catherine turned

to Rosie. "If you tell her we earn half-a-crown and more she'd get very suspicious. That's a lot of money. She'd know Foley was up to something."

"What do *you* think he's up to, Catherine?"

"What he said. He wants to stop these men acting against him and his friends."

"How will he do that? Will he go to the police?"

Catherine was scornful, "The polis? He wouldn't trust them! The DMPs work for the crown, not for the likes of us. Foley and his pals will probably take the law into their own hands and challenge McClean and his friends to a fight, get their own back that way."

She was so matter-of-fact Rosie was comforted. Then she said, "Are the DMPs the same as the police?"

"You *have* to see a doctor!" Her friend's face was furrowed with concern. "Your ambrosia is getting worse. Every dog in the street knows the Dublin Metropolitan Police. They're all huge. You can't miss those big helmets with the spikes. Even Rip Van Winkle'd recognise a DMP."

Annoyed at the comparison, Rosie forgot herself. "Well, Rip Van Winkle didn't have amnesia! He ended up in a future he didn't know, not a past. There's a big difference between sleeping for twenty years and going back more than seventy! OK, things were different for him, but this is like another planet to me – "

Catherine's jaw dropped and Rosie stopped. She'd gone too far this time. Across the table her friend was trying to make sense of what she'd said. For a moment Rosie was tempted to tell her the truth. But Catherine might well think she was mad. Plus she might tell Lilian, making her even more uneasy and suspicious. Rosie wanted to be friends with her grandmother. The truth would only scare and aggravate her and neither she nor Catherine would believe it anyway.

So Rosie looked at her friend's bewildered face and smiled. "I'm rambling, amn't I? You would too if you had amnesia. Everything is so strange, it *does* feel like a different planet or a different time. It's so frustrating!"

Catherine was very understanding. "Poor you! You must feel like a stranger. It's because of your . . . your . . . *amnesia*." She pronounced the word carefully and triumphantly.

"Still, things are getting better," Rosie reassured her. "I know now what a DMP is and I remember everything that happened since we met." Her face darkened. "That's why I worry about McClean and his friends and what Foley might do to them. I like McClean."

"Don't you like Foley, too?"

She thought about it and nodded. She did like Foley. She liked the knack he had of making her feel important. He made it plain she impressed him, in spite of her grubby appearance. He had treated her and Catherine as equals, which McClean's posh friends had not done. He'd made her laugh with his lunatic antics over the photo. When he smiled he looked no older than her cousin Shane. He was generous, too, and funny like Shane.

"What are you worried about, Rosie? Foley is a decent fellow!"

Rosie fervently hoped her friend was right.

The streets were quiet when they set off for the hospital. The lamplight was hazy and soft. Everywhere there were shadows. Pedestrians hurried. On the side roads there was no traffic and the silence was eerie. Rosie was glad to reach Sackville Street where the trams were running and some of the shops still open.

She was mesmerised by Findlater's window. Huge tins of Jacob's biscuits took pride of place among open sacks of spices, displays of cooked meats, jars of preserves and bottles of wine. The aroma of good things was heady. Rosie had a sudden desire to eat something more exciting than the bread and dripping, bread and jam and bread and spam Catherine thought were such wonderful treats. Pressing her head against the window, she dreamed of curries, of spaghetti bolognese smothered in parmesan cheese, sweet and sour pork, lasagne and lemon chicken. The minute she got home she would eat all of her favourite dishes!

Pulling her across the road, past the Carlton cinema, Catherine said they had to hurry. "The hospital is very strict about visiting hours."

Turning down Henry Street, Rosie wished she'd more time to look in the shop windows. But now Catherine was almost running and she followed suit, noticing on her way a child drawing curtains in an upstairs window and behind her a man sitting in an armchair by the fire. People seemed to be living over the shops, she thought, and wondered what it would be like to grow up in the hustle and bustle of Henry Street.

The hospital fascinated Rosie. Nurses glided along the dimly-lit corridors, wearing bonnets and crisp white aprons over a long dark uniform dress, the image of Florence Nightingale in a picture Rosie had once seen. Now and again a patient was trundled by in an old-fashioned wheelchair, the wheels huge and spindly. Doctors looked all important in high starched collars and impeccable suits under white coats. One of them loftily directed them to a dormitory ward which, it seemed to Rosie, contained at least forty beds. She stared at the two long rows of patients thinking they looked as if they were neatly stuffed into matchboxes.

"Over here, Rosie!" Catherine had found her mother.

Rosie blinked. She looked too young to be anyone's mother. Her fair hair was loose about her shoulders and her thin narrow frame in the white cotton nightdress was childlike. She was grinning away at her daughter, who grinned back delightedly.

"You look so much better, Mother! This is my friend Rosie. She's staying with me while you're here."

Mrs Dalton shook her hand. "You're very welcome. And of course you can stay as long as you like."

Rosie marvelled. Mom would have asked a thousand questions before she welcomed a stranger. "You can't be too careful these days," was her favourite phrase. But in the tenement everyone except Lilian treated her as a friend.

"We're managing grand," Catherine said, in answer to her mother's next question. "We got a job doing messages for the Gresham." She winked at Rosie, who took the hint to say nothing about Foley.

Mrs Dalton breathed in the fragrance of the flowers they'd bought from the street vendor outside the hospital. "Beautiful," she murmured, "just what I needed to cheer me up."

Catherine was alarmed, "You are feeling better, Mother? You look so well."

"I'm feeling perfect. Doctor Sullivan did all the tests. I don't have TB. There was nothing wrong with me except tiredness and worry." Her face was grave. "I suppose there's no news of your father?"

"No, Mother."

Seeing her daughter's dejected face, Mrs Dalton became resolute. "He was to stay in the Catholic Working Men's club in Manchester. I'll write to them the minute I get home. If I hadn't been so weary, I'd have done so weeks ago."

"You don't think he's in trouble?" For a moment Catherine was the one who looked ill.

"There has to be some reason why he hasn't contacted us. Your father would never desert us. We must face it, Catherine, there's something wrong and I'm going to find out what it is. I'm only sorry to have been such a heavy burden on you. But that will all change when I get home."

"You weren't well, Mother. I didn't mind – " Then Catherine's eyes filled and she had trouble speaking. "You think Father's dead, don't you?"

"I do not! I'd know if he were dead."

She spoke with such conviction and finality that they believed her.

"Doctor Sullivan says I can leave on Monday. But I won't go home in an ambulance. You can meet me here at 11 o'clock."

On the way home, in the emptiness of Great Britain Street, it dawned on Rosie that someone was following them. She looked around and saw a shadow slip into a doorway. A moment later the footsteps resumed, though she had to strain to hear them. "Stop," she murmured to Catherine. The follower stopped too, starting again when they did. Whoever it was kept a steady pace behind them, content to stay at a certain distance. At North Great George's Street the footsteps ceased.

"Thank heavens," Rosie muttered, but turning round she could make out the figure of a man in a belted overcoat watching them. He moved and for a moment she saw his face in the lamplight. Then he slipped back into the shadows.

They were glad to get into the tenement, to hear the movements and voices of their neighbours. With some relief they closed the door of their room. Now they were safe and whoever it was would surely go away. He had left it too late to attack or rób them. But when they peered out the window, they saw their pursuer standing directly below, under the streetlight, staring up at them. In a panic they clutched each other.

"What if he comes up here?" Rosie said, "He might be a murderer! Let's lock the door!"

"There is no lock. Oh, God. He looks so mean and vicious!"

The man's lips twisted in a sneer as he registered their fear. They had never seen him before, but knew his intentions were not good . . . yet in their terror they could not move away from the window.

Within minutes two Crossley tenders screeched to a halt outside. They saw the man talk to an officer and point towards them. Catherine recovered her wits first. "Move, Rosie! Down to the Hennesseys."

All through the house neighbours knocked on walls and beat the chimneybreasts with pokers to signal the Tans' arrival. Anyone with anything to hide did so as fast as possible.

Catherine had second thoughts. "There's no time to get out. We must hide your kit-bag and camera! Get them quickly." Already the Tans were pounding up the stairs and separating into pairs to raid the rooms. Like lightening, Catherine crossed again to the window and, tugging at the wooden sill, lifted it to reveal a deep space that went under the floorboards. Seizing the

119

knapsack and camera she stuffed them out of sight, then crossed to sit down opposite Rosie at the table.

The door burst open. Two men in khaki uniform and dark green caps confronted them, pistols drawn, faces shiny with sweat and twitching with excitement.

"We want to see you!" the smaller of the two announced brusquely, his eyes narrowing with menace. He was waving his gun about as though conducting an orchestra. The girls could make no response, intent on the weaving pistol and wondering which way they should duck.

"Did you hear what we said?" He was snarling.

"Eh . . . yes." Catherine answered him calmly in spite of the waving gun. "You said you wanted to see us. Well, now you've seen us maybe you could leave before that gun goes off."

"You cheeky blackguard!" The small soldier was appalled by this lack of respect. So was Rosie, especially since the gun was now waving about even faster. The other soldier was quite still, his pistol down at his side. She became uncomfortably aware that he was staring at her. Looking at him properly for the first time, she gasped.

He was the one who had saluted her from the back of the lorry!

Anger had replaced fear in Catherine. "Cheeky blackguard? What a nerve! You've no right to be here waving weapons at us in our own home. You're the cheeky blackguard!"

The soldier's eyes became slits and steadying his hand he took aim at Catherine.

Rosie dived out of her seat and under the table, but Catherine didn't move. Afterwards she claimed she couldn't, she was stuck to the chair with fright. At the time, Rosie thought it was lunatic courage and, gripping her friend's leg, tried to pull her down. She might as well have been tugging at a sack of lead.

"Don't fire, mate! They're only kids." It was the other Tan. But from her crouched position, Rosie saw his companion level the gun at Catherine's head and close one eye for a better shot. The girl's face drained and she swayed. His partner turned in disbelief, about to intervene.

"Pop!" the small man said and laughed.

How dare he! Rosie was seething. The thick little fool! she thought. The coward! A flamin' bully with a gun, playing games with people's lives and laughing at them.

"*Sap!*" She yelled, rage propelling her from under the table across the room, straight into the soldier.

Her action had bowled him over and his cap fell over his eyes. Rosie kicked him hard on the rear end. "I hate you!" The other soldier stood by, too surprised or unwilling to help.

The noise of a gunshot brought Rosie to her senses. My God, was she hit? Was Catherine? A shower of chalky plaster told her the bullet had struck the ceiling.

Rosie stood back, all courage gone. She would have fallen, but Catherine gripped her arm.

"What on earth is going on here? Corporal Brown, why are you rolling around? And why did you fire that gun? Get up at once, man, and answer me!"

In the doorway, a tall officer in a dark blue uniform looked scornfully at the heap on the floor.

Corporal Brown struggled to his feet. "It was not my fault, sir! I was attacked, knocked over and savagely kicked by this hooligan, which is why my gun went off, sir."

His captain's scorn deepened. "Attacked? Savagely kicked? By this youngster? An armed soldier in His Majesty's service! You are pathetic, Brown. Now get out, the two of you. Stand guard outside the door, just in case this brutal ruffian decides to turn on me." He eyed Rosie with cold amusement. Brown got to his feet, his face dark with rage. He said nothing.

When the door closed the officer got down to business immediately. "What were you two doing on Morehampton Road? Why did you deliver the post to number 117? Why did you go back again? What did the note you were carrying yesterday mean?" Neither girl answered though he let the silence hang a long while. Forced to break it himself, his irritation was obvious. "I could have you arrested for attacking one of my men. I could have you brought away in one of the lorries. You might never come back. Or I could let Brown back in here with you. He's a bad loser. Quite vicious. And you made him look ridiculous in front of his commanding officer."

They shivered. The captain spoke as if he were trying to work out the best option.

"Brown is ridiculous!" Rosie murmured.

The officer shrugged. "That doesn't stop him killing. He enjoys it. He even has a favourite method. Which is why his nickname is 'Bayonet Brown'."

He was telling the truth, they knew. Brown had revelled in terrifying them.

"We were on Morehampton Road selling statues." Catherine sounded weary of the whole business. "You can ask at the other houses. The maid in number 100 might remember us. We delivered letters to 117 because the postman asked us to. He had arranged to meet his girl and he was late. You can check with him too. Satisfied?"

"Not yet. Tell me why you went back – and what that note meant. Then maybe I'll be satisfied."

This time Rosie answered. "We made money there. What other reason could we have for going back?" She spoke impatiently, as if explaining the obvious to an idiot. "And we don't know what the note meant because Catherine had only just picked it off the ground when that fool stopped us."

The officer gaped at her. Who was she calling a fool?

"If you are referring to Captain McClean, it would be wise to show more respect!"

"Well, he didn't respect Catherine, did he?" Rosie was peeved. "He twisted her arm until it hurt. That's why we ran away from him."

"But you turned up at his house again."

Rosie remained steady. "It's hard to remember who lives in which house, especially when it's only your second visit. He gave me a terrible fright, so he did, charging after me like a bull!"

"But you asked for him by name!"

"Only because when the door opened I knew it was his house. The hall had dark red wallpaper. I was afraid then he might be in." Rosie prayed that the captain was as ignorant as herself about the colour of the wallpaper.

He must have been for he made no comment, looking at them in silence for a moment, testing out what they'd said. It added up except for one thing. "How do I know you're not lying about finding the note? It was, after all, in code and marked 'urgent'. No one would have been so careless as to lose something so important."

For a second they were stumped, then Catherine had a brain-wave. "If *I'd* been given an urgent message like that," she said carefully, "I'd have kept it in my pocket, not carried it in my hand where someone like McClean might see it. The only reason it was in my hand was because I'd just picked it up."

Perfect! Rosie breathed a sigh of relief.

The captain bit his lip, pondering. Then he said, "If you two are lying, you will regret it." He walked to the window and signalled. Below, the lorries began to rev up.

In the flickering candlelight, silhouetted against the glass, the officer was like a shadow from the past. He turned, his face pale as a ghost. "If this is treachery," he said, "it can only end in death."

He strode to the door. Outside the two Tans stood to attention while he went downstairs, barking orders at his men to follow him. Corporal Brown turned to Rosie. "I never forget a face!" he sneered.

I don't either, Rosie thought, but in your case I'll definitely try!

Unable to think of anything else, Brown glared and followed his captain.

The other soldier smiled at them. "He deserved everything he got. I admire your guts."

Catherine stared at him, stony-faced. Before the door closed, Rosie saw the smile disappear and his young face become weary again.

Catherine was jubilant. "We are *so* lucky, Rosie. That officer could have looked in my pockets and found they were just holes. He'd have realised then why I had the note in my hand!"

Chapter 11

THE TENEMENT was bursting with excitement when the Tans left. Word went around that the Dalton child and her pal were brutally treated by "that scum." Shots had been fired and desperate threats made.

In no time at all rumour replaced truth and neighbours crowded the stairs to see "the bodies of those poor young ones, riddled with bullets by the unnatural and atrocious Tans."

Not a bit put out at the sight of the corpses in the full of their health, they listened eagerly to Catherine's tale. The girls became the heroes of the hour. The neighbours were particularly gripped by Rosie's attack on Corporal Brown and their praise was fulsome.

"Aren't you the daredevil now, to be lashin' into the likes of him."

"I've often wanted to kick a Tan in the bum, but sure I'd never have the nerve!"

"Brown! He's a well-known savage. But you showed him, Rosie. He won't pretend to shoot anyone again!"

No, he'll just kill them outright next time, Rosie thought. She was dismayed. Another neighbour reinforced her fear. "You want to watch out for Brown. He's an evil character and he won't take this lying down."

Someone sniggered, "Oh, but the boyo *did* take it lying down. Didn't she knock him over before she booted his bum! Good on you, I say, though indeed you better keep an eye out. You're a goner if that fella gets the chance. He's a self-important bowsie and he won't like being a laughing-stock!"

Rosie groaned, remembering the captain's observation that Brown could not stand humiliation. It was the man's own fault. He shouldn't aim loaded guns at people's heads and shout "Pop!"

Really, the old days were gross! Rotten food, rotten clothes, no proper lighting, no comfort, no toilets and demented thugs pretending to shoot people. She was not looking forward to the rest of the week, especially Sunday. She thought of the violence ahead, of the panic and mayhem. She thought of her doubts about Foley. She thought of Catherine, fearful for her future.

Now, on top of all these worries, she had to "keep an eye out" for a lunatic who could kill her and get away with it.

Give me the nineties any day! she decided.

On Thursday morning when they called to the Gresham, Rosie wanted to tell Foley about the raid and was disappointed to find he'd been and gone.

"He left a message," William said. "You're to go round to 'The Republican Outfitters' on Talbot Street. A man is expecting you there."

They had no trouble finding the small poky premises but got a great shock when they saw the person behind the counter. It was Foley's friend, Clancy, from Morehampton Road.

"What are you doing here? We thought you were keeping an eye on McClean!" Rosie said.

"I own this shop. And keep your voice down."

"Sure, there's no one else in here," Catherine said.

"Walls have ears!" Clancy was whispering. Fed up with this melodrama, Rosie began to wonder was he a bit simple. She whispered back, "Not only walls, Mr Clancy. What about floors and ceilings? What about that counter and those windows . . . do they have ears too?"

He straightened up and stared, then turned to Catherine. "Your friend's not all there. Not the full shilling at all."

"She got a blow on the head." Catherine sounded weary.

"He started it!" Rosie muttered, furious.

"I have a job for you," he addressed Catherine, "if your friend is up to it." He studied them a moment. "Those are grand jackets you have. Lovely. Fine big pockets!"

Definitely loopy, Rosie thought but said nothing.

"Mine are full of holes," Catherine pulled them out to show him.

Rosie sighed. She was among simpletons.

"What state are yours in?" Clancy's enquiry was anxious.

"Absolutely fabulous!" Rosie kept her face serious. "You've never seen such lining! And a wonderful colour. Any collector would be mad about them."

Clancy blinked. "Did they let your friend out for the day?" he asked Catherine. "Pocket collectors! All I want to know is whether she has holes in them."

"He's not normal!" Rosie decided she too would talk through Catherine. "Normal persons don't go round asking about the state of your pockets."

"Her pockets are fine, Mr Clancy. Perfect. She minds all our money in them."

127

Clancy continued, "Foley wanted me to send you note-carrying again, but I think we can put those fine pockets to better use. Are you with me? There's ten bob in it for you."

He was speaking in rigmaroles. Rosie wanted nothing more to do with him. But Catherine had heard the magic words "ten bob" and was ecstatic.

"Whatever you want, Mr Clancy!" she breathed. "We're with you."

"Good woman!" He slapped a ten-shilling note on the counter. "Here's what you do. At half past two this afternoon you're to be waiting on the corner at the end of Lower Abbey Street. I'll come up to you – " he nodded at Rosie " – and drop one or two things in your pocket. Give no indication that anything has happened. When I've disappeared, go to the Gresham. Foley will be there. Give him my little packages and tell him I changed plans."

Rosie wanted to ask a few questions. She wanted to tell him they might be followed. He should know about Corporal Brown.

But Catherine had taken the money and was now bundling her out of the shop.

Once outside Rosie protested, "We ought to have told him we could be followed!"

"Have you noticed anyone after us? Can you see anyone now?"

"No. But that might just mean they're very clever. They could be setting a trap."

Catherine laughed. "Well, they weren't very clever the last time. You could hear that fella a mile away. He was so obvious, the way he kept ducking into doorways, then standing under the lamp for everyone to see. He couldn't have passed any spying exams!"

"Maybe they wanted us to see him," Rosie said slowly. "Maybe they wanted to frighten us into giving them information. And they're being more sneaky now 'cos that didn't work."

"I'll say it didn't work!" Catherine giggled, remembering Browne's face after Rosie's attack. "But if we told Clancy about the raid he wouldn't give us the job and we'd get no ten bob."

She was blind to everything except money and Rosie was furious. "That stupid money is all you care about, isn't it? A measly ten bob! It's only worth fifty pence, but you'd do anything for it!"

She was sorry as soon as she'd said it, but Catherine took no offence. Instead, she was concerned. "I think maybe you're deranged, Rosie." She was deadly earnest. "Ten shillings is worth one hundred and twenty pence, not fifty. You shouldn't be let out with money if you think it's fifty! That's only four shilling and tuppence! Janey, Rosie your brain is addled so . . ."

"Shut up! Stop going on about money. This job could be dangerous!"

"No, it couldn't. All Clancy wants to do is slip a couple of packages in your pocket. He probably hasn't time to give them to Foley himself."

She made it sound so simple, Rosie lost some of her fear. She felt ashamed of herself when Catherine added, "When Mother comes out of hospital she's going to need nice food, fruit and vegetables. The money will be useful."

Her friend worried about money only because she had so little. Whatever she managed to acquire she always shared.

By 2.25 they were in place, wondering from which direction Clancy would arrive. They tried to look as if

129

they'd bumped into each other and had a lot of chat to catch up on.

Their conversation faltered when they heard gunfire. Three shots rang out. Instinctively, passers-by stopped and everyone ducked. Someone shouted, "It's the bank! The Dublin Savings Bank!"

Three men came bounding down the steps of the bank, waving guns. No one else on the street moved as the gunmen took off in different directions. One grabbed a bike from against the railings and made for O'Connell Street. A second man disappeared down an alleyway and the third raced in their direction.

Rosie came to life. "Run, Catherine! He's waving a gun!" She turned but Catherine gripped her. "It's Clancy!"

Frozen, they stared as Clancy hurtled towards them. He brushed against Rosie and she felt a double weight drop into her pocket. "Go! Go! Go!" He yelled.

They went. "Not with me!" He snarled and stopped. "Remember your orders!" They were around the corner. "And don't run. Walk!" He straightened his tie, adjusted his overcoat and, taking his own advice, sauntered away from them.

The girls found walking almost impossible. Every time they slowed down panic gripped them and they began to run again. Rosie was too afraid to put a hand in her pocket. What she wanted now, more than anything, was to reach Foley. Foley would get rid of this terror. He would make things safe.

He was pacing up and down the kitchen of the hotel when they arrived. "I expected you sooner," he said. "I had to rush off this morning. Did Clancy give you the note?" Then he saw their faces. "What happened?"

Rosie took the gun out of her pocket. "Clancy gave us a different job," she said.

"Are you telling me . . . ? Did that fool . . . ? Did he involve you . . . ?" He could not formulate what he wanted to say. Rosie put the gun on the table. She felt in her pocket again, took out the bulky brown-paper bag and handed it over. Foley looked inside. His face paled. "You could have been killed. That lunatic – he's dangerous! He had no right . . ."

Curious, Catherine and Rosie looked into the bag. They saw wads of money.

"Clancy will get us all killed." Foley went even whiter and his eyes began to glitter.

"What if someone saw what he did and came after you?"

Rosie swallowed. It was time to tell him everything: how they'd been followed home from the hospital, how the Tans had raided the tenement, and especially how Brown had threatened them. She had hardly finished when Foley started pushing them towards the door. "Quick!" he said, "Out! If someone *is* following you, then he'll have seen you with Clancy and you can be sure all he's waiting for is reinforcements before coming in here!"

He took up the gun from the table. Rosie was already opening the door to the lane. She was first out and saw a flash as a bullet went over her head and someone shouted "Stop! Or I'll shoot!" She recognised Corporal Brown's voice and was paralysed. Behind her, Foley pulled Catherine back into the kitchen and murmured to the terrified Rosie, "You'll be all right. Don't run."

She couldn't run. Transfixed in the alley by Brown's approaching steps, her only comfort was Foley's low voice. "I won't let him hurt you, Rosie. Back away from him when he gets near the door. I promise he won't harm you."

131

He stopped talking. In the kitchen no one breathed. Outside in the shadowy lane, Rosie saw Brown's face twist in triumph. He walked slowly towards her, savouring her terror. "Thought you could make me look a fool, did you? Have everybody laughing?" He stopped and raised his rifle, grinning. "Don't think I'm going to waste another bullet on you. No. I've something more interesting in store for you, Miss."

She watched him fix a bayonet to the barrel and at last she did as Foley said. She thought at any moment her legs would buckle as she inched her way back. "Courage, Rosie." Foley's words were barely audible but they helped.

Now Brown was a fraction away from the door.

It was then she saw another figure, framed in the entrance to the lane. It was Brown's partner, the Tan who had saluted her. He raised his gun and shouted, "Don't you touch her, you murdering swine!"

Everything accelerated then. Brown turned around, startled, then swung back as Foley yanked him through the door. "Quick, Rosie! In and lock the door!" he yelled. She rushed inside and slid the bolt into place.

Foley had the Tan pinned against the wall. The rifle clattered to the floor and Brown was gabbling with fright. "Don't hurt me! Please, sir! I meant no harm. Just wanted to teach her a lesson. Please, sir!"

"You're lying. Even your pal knew you were going to kill her!" Face set, Foley's right hand clenched into a fist and Rosie knew he was going to smash it into the Tan's face. Drawn by the hullabaloo, Hugh Callaghan rushed into the kitchen, followed by William.

"Are you mad?" Mr Callaghan roared. "Do you want to bring the whole murdering pack down on this hotel? Let him go, man!"

"He was going to bayonet Rosie." Foley's face was only an inch away from Brown's and he ground the words out, daring the Tan to deny them. "This cowardly scum was ready to kill her!" Brown said nothing. His eyes were closed and Rosie thought he might faint with terror.

"But he didn't kill her, did he? So let him go." Mr Callaghan sounded calm, even authoritative.

Foley stepped away. The Tan did not move. "Look at me!" Foley said and Brown did as he was told. "I *know* you. I *know* your name. It's famous. 'Bayonet Brown'. Called after your favourite weapon. You like to run people through, don't you? So you can watch their agony."

The Tan had trouble breathing now. His eyes were locked by Foley's and he shuddered when his enemy suddenly retrieved his rifle from the floor and pointed the blade at him. For a moment Rosie thought he was going to use it. Instead he turned it around and offered the rifle to Brown. It was some seconds before the Tan's hand stopped trembling long enough for him to grip it.

"Remember what I said. I know you. If *ever* you come near these kids again, you won't live long enough to regret it. Do you hear me?"

Brown nodded and swallowed. Coolly, Foley turned away, exposing his back to the bayonet. Brown straightened and there was a collective gasp. All of them thought Foley was finished. Instead the bolt was jerked back and Brown was out the door.

Hugh Callaghan was puzzled. "There must be more of them out there. They never travel alone. Where's the reinforcements?"

"There was only his partner," Rosie said. "And he wouldn't call for help. Not for Brown."

"How do you know?"

"I just do."

The others did not share her certainty. "If reinforcements do come," Hugh Callaghan said, "It will be safer for all of us if William and I say we never saw you three before and we don't know a thing about you. After all, I stopped you, Foley, from harming Brown, so they just might believe me. But you'd better stay away from the hotel for a while."

"Good advice," Foley nodded. "Anyway, my groundwork is done here. I won't be in these kitchens again."

They made their way through the warren of lanes. Before he left them, Foley turned to Catherine and Rosie. He was hesitant, awkward. "Look, I'm sorry for what Clancy did. He shouldn't have involved you in anything so dangerous. You'll be glad to know, Rosie, I don't need you for any more jobs. The few loose ends I can tie up myself."

But at that moment Rosie wasn't glad. Foley had rescued her from death. The last few days had been the most exciting of her life. She would miss that excitement.

Catherine felt the same way. "Those jobs were very interesting."

He smiled. "*Interesting!* It's not exactly the word I'd have used for getting your arm twisted and helping bank robbers. Not to mention being chased by maniacs like Brown."

"Will we see you again?" Catherine was wistful. Life would be very boring without Foley.

"In a few days time, you won't want to know me." His eyes were sombre. "You'll think I'm a villain."

Rosie shook her head. "No, I won't. You saved my life – I'll always remember that."

"Well, I won't forget you two either. And who knows, Rosie, in years to come we might even be friends."

Rosie was silent. Foley thanked them for their help and said goodbye. After a few yards his step became jaunty and he turned. "Remember, the future belongs to us!" he called.

But not the same future. The thought made Rosie sad.

Chapter 12

THEY DID not wake till ten o'clock on Friday. The day was glorious, sunlight brightening even the darkest corners of the room. She stood at the window basking in the unseasonal warmth.

The street was busy. Women called to each other as they hung the washing on window poles. Below, mothers wheeled babies in rickety perambulators. Men had already gathered at the corner for a smoke and a game of pitch-and-toss. Her great-uncles were among groups of boys playing football, kicking a tightly-tied parcel of newspaper, the goals marked by jackets and jumpers. On the pavement a small girl was trying to whip a wooden spinning top into action.

The free day beckoned.

Catherine was full of plans. "We'll go to Grafton Street, see all the toffs and have lemonade and buns in Fry's café. And we can go to the pictures. Charlie Chaplin's on in the Sackville. Or we can see Lily Jacobson in the Carlton."

Silent movies! Rosie gave a silent scream.

They called to see Lilian before setting off. For once she was welcoming. "Come in. Mother's gone for the messages and I'm the only one here." She looked shyly at Rosie. "I heard what you did on Wednesday night," she said. "You were very brave!" Rosie blushed with pleasure. Her grandmother was eager to make up for past unfriendliness. "I'm sorry I was horrible to you. You were right. I was jealous because the two of you are having such a good time while I'm stuck in."

Remembering how excluded she'd felt when her cousins went to the States without her, Rosie was sympathetic. "Once you're better, you'll be able to come out with us."

"I *am* better. Mother is afraid I'll get sick again if I set foot outside the door. But at least she's promised I can go to Croke Park on Sunday."

Rosie tried to look pleased. "Great! It's a pity you can't spend today with us. We have loads of money – " She listed their plans and Lilian's eyes grew round. "Maybe I will come with you . . . though Mother will kill me . . ."

"We'll say we persuaded you. You should come!" Catherine was encouraging, "You really do look better, Lilian. Oh, come on! We'll have a wonderful day and this evening, when she sees you're fine, she'll stop worrying and say nothing. You can leave a message for her with your brother Joseph."

Lilian made one condition. "I'd love to see Lily Jacobson. Can we go to the Carlton?" They nodded and she gave in. "Let's go now, immediately, in case Mother comes back."

They dived out the door and down the stairs two at a time until they were on the street. Pausing only to tell Joseph, they sped around the corner, not slowing till they reached North Frederick Street. Rosie saw no sign of Brown or anyone else who might be following them.

"Yahoo!" Lilian yelled. "Yahoodyhoo!" She was like a prisoner released from jail. Eyes shining, she linked the other two and skipped in her clumsy boots along Sackville Street. A well-dressed woman clicked her tongue and frowned. In a perfect imitation Lilian did the same back, even repeating haughtily, "Definitely *not* young ladies!"

They giggled as the woman flounced away.

Lilian was eager for fun. "Let's get a chase," she said, "from that fella there."

"That fella there" was a large policeman standing at a lamppost. Hands clasped behind his back, rocking back and forward on his heels, he was the lord of all he surveyed. Before they knew it, Lilian had raced over to him, jumped up and tipped off his helmet. Unfortunately the spike whacked his foot and he abandoned all dignity. "Aaagh!" he yelled, clutching the injured toes and hopping around the helmet, his face twisted in torture.

"Doing a war dance, constable?" a passing smart alec inquired.

Pain gave way to rage. "Who did that? Who smacked my helmet? It is an offence to assault an officer of the law or to interfere with his property. I shall arrest the criminal at once!"

Immediately the small gathering evaporated, leaving only the three grinning twelve-year-olds. He lurched towards them. "It was one of you. Come here! At once!"

But wisely they raced away. He limped after them, furiously blowing his whistle and shouting, "Halt! Hooligans!"

They took off across O'Connell Bridge, Lilian whooping with joy. In D'Olier Street they rested, leaning against a shop window, laughing and gasping for breath.

Rosie saw Lilian with new eyes. Her granny the cop basher! *And* she'd robbed Findlater's in 1916. This was the nice old lady who liked bridge parties. The one who sometimes sniffed and said, "The youth of today have no respect for their elders."

Really, adults are always pretending they were perfect children, Rosie thought. But the next time Gran gives out to me, I'm going to tell her "at least I never assaulted a policeman or interfered with his property! And I never looted shops, either."

"Look at this!" Catherine urged. Rosie turned to see a wonderland. They were outside the Junior Army and Navy Stores and in the window were the kind of toys she had only ever seen on the Antique Road Show. There were wooden scooters, model Chevrolet motorcars, old-fashioned dolls and mechanical soldiers drawn up in colourful regiments.

Her eyes were drawn to the clockwork Punch and Judy show at the front of the window. A vicious-looking Punch was battering a policeman. "He's just like you, Lilian," she observed. They giggled and made their way companionably to Grafton Street.

Riveted at the sight of the most extraordinary knickers she'd ever seen, Rosie stopped outside Roberts' drapery shop. A female figure was wearing a huge pair of what the advertisement called 'trunk knickers', in a vile shade of green, elasticated at the waist and ankles.

You probably *could* fit a trunk into them! Rosie mused.

Catherine followed her gaze. "I wish I could afford those," she said.

"And you think my head is damaged!" Rosie muttered, but not loudly enough for her friend to hear.

"They'd keep us lovely and warm," Catherine sighed.

But something even worse distracted Rosie. Another shop dummy was wearing a sort of straitjacket. Made of a sickly orange material and thickly ridged, it stretched from her ribs to a few inches above her knees. Rosie studied the notice in front of the dummy:

We proudly present the latest whalebone corset for discerning and fashionable ladies.

"Does anyone wear those things?" She pointed.

"Of course," Catherine said. "You have to wear them when you're older."

"Why?"

"Because you have to. That's why. Every woman does."

"No, they don't!" Rosie knew for certain Gran didn't. Neither did Mom.

"Yes, they do!" The other two chorused with equal conviction.

"When you get older," Catherine dredged up another reason, "you get a *huge* wobbly stomach and a corset holds it in. Only whalebones are strong enough for the job."

"You mean they kill real whales?" Rosie was shocked.

"What else would have whalebones, stupid?"

Rosie studied the ridiculous-looking article in the window. "You couldn't even run in it," she said.

"Women don't run," Catherine sighed. Some day Rosie'd get better, but meantime it was hard to put up with all the blank spaces in her brain.

Rosie thought of Mom's latest keep-fit campaign, jogging every day in her track suit. She was in training for the Dublin marathon next year. Lucky she didn't have to wear a corset!

They strolled along Grafton Street. Rosie recognised Switzers and Brown Thomas, but that was all. She was transfixed by novelties: by the glass jars in *Nobletts' Confectioners*, filled with coconut creams, nougat delight and Peggy's legs; by the colourful baubles in Woolworth's 3d and 6d store. She stared at the plush exterior of *Maison Prost, Coiffeur and Perfumier* and wondered what kind of Aladdin's cave was inside.

"You have to be very rich to get your hair styled there," Lilian told her. A hairdresser's! The magic faded until she reached Freke's window and read the gold lettering: "Artistic Oriental fabric. Eastern wares and textiles." The window displayed opulent silks and rugs, luxurious ottomans and richly-embroidered wall hangings. She could have stood for hours but the others dragged her away.

Delicious aromas made her hungry. They were outside Fry's café. Catherine studied the menu on the billboard. "We can have lemonade and a gateau each."

A cross middle-aged man barred their entrance. "Where do you think you are going? *You* may not come in!" To Rosie's astonishment, the other two turned on their heels. She stood her ground.

"Why not? Why can't we come in?"

The glance he gave her was full of contempt. "Because I am the manager and I say so. And because this is not a beggars' hostel. Our establishment is for respectable customers only."

Rosie's face grew hot with anger. "We're not beggars. We can pay for our food."

He raised an eyebrow. "Then I suggest you pay for it elsewhere. We do not welcome people who look as if they might be more at home in a dustbin. Now if you will kindly leave the premises – "

"I will not!"

"Come on, Rosie. He'll only call the polis." The

141

other two tugged at her jacket. Rosie recognised defeat. She thought about giving the horrible snob a kick and running. Then she noticed a well-dressed man with a monocle who had stopped to listen on his way out. Another snob, Rosie thought and was just about to snap "What are you gawking at?" when he spoke.

"Surely, Mr Massey, you are not preventing these children entering the café?"

Mr Massey looked uncomfortable.

"He is, Mister. He called us beggars. He said we live in a dustbin. But we don't, do we?"

Catherine and Lilian looked startled at the question. They shook their heads vigorously.

Seeing a few more customers and encouraged by the gentleman's sympathy, Rosie went on sorrowfully, "He's not a nice man. It's not our fault we're poor."

A couple of people looked accusingly at Mr Massey who reddened.

"Indeed it's not your fault," the gentleman stated, "and if Mr Massey does not allow you the same rights as other paying customers I shall no longer have any dealings with this establishment."

The manager crawled instantly. "A misunderstanding, Mr Yeats, I do assure you. These children are most welcome and as a gesture of goodwill their refreshments will be at our expense. I shall see to them personally. Come this way, please."

Seizing Rosie by the arm he practically frogmarched her to a table, then pushed her into a chair. The other two sat happily beside her.

Mr Yeats was still standing in the doorway. The manager waved and gave him a sickly smile, then stuck the menu under Rosie's nose. Calmly she ordered lemonade and gateaux. They beamed at Mr Yeats, who waited until they were served. His name was vaguely familiar to Rosie. He must be quite an important man, she thought.

The girls ate ravenously. But Rosie saw how out of place they looked. Everyone else was well-dressed in clothes that fitted. She noticed how grimy the three of them were. The tenement had no bath or hot water, only one sink on the landing that sixty people had to share. It was impossible to wash properly.

No one else in the restaurant crammed the food into their mouths. She saw people looking at them and pretending not to. When Catherine and Lilian finished eating they too noticed the stares. Not even Rosie wanted to stay any longer.

She had gone to the Carlton cinema with Mom and Dad once before it closed down. It was old and musty, she'd thought then, with dust rising from the seats when they sat down. Now, as she entered the lobby, she was astonished at how lavish it was. The deep burgundy carpet matched the flock wallpaper, brightened by magnificent gilt mirrors and the framed black-and-white photographs of stars Rosie had never heard of, except for Charlie Chaplin.

The attendant was a man of impressive build, wearing a blue and gold uniform, a hard peaked hat with a gold band and white gloves. Rosie was sure he would throw them out but he never gave them a second glance. In the centre of the lobby a free-standing billboard announced:

SHOWING NOW:
A DAUGHTER OF THE EAST
FEATURING MISS LILY JACOBSON
A FASCINATING DRAMA OF THE EAST

A PICTURE OF GREAT BEAUTY AND ABSORBING HEART INTEREST
SPECIAL MUSIC PROGRAMME PLAYED BY MISTER E GOLDWATER
FROM CARMEN AND FANTASIA

Included was a startling photograph of the star. "She has two black eyes! She looks as if she's been in a boxing match," Rosie said.

"She does not!" Lilian sprang to the actress's defence. "She's beautiful, so she is. Her eyes are just dark and mysterious."

Catherine paid three shillings at the mahogany counter and they were each given a programme as well as their ticket. The attendant marched before them into the cinema and, with a wave of his hand, indicated their seats.

The picture house was three times bigger than Rosie remembered it. The seats were as large as armchairs. A grand piano stood below the screen, sheet music in place, the top open. A man in a morning suit approached and, with a flourish of his coat tails, sat down to play. The cinema was half-full when the electric lights went out and the picture began.

"She *has* black eyes," Rosie muttered. The story unfolded to the poignant music of the pianist. A story of hopeless love. Rosie laughed all the way through the film. The other two were mortified. "Will you shut up!" It only made her worse. On screen the heroine sighed and wept, mopped her brow and fainted, all with great melodrama and no voice. In the end she died of a broken heart. Her black eyes fluttered with pain for five minutes before they closed forever.

Rosie stuffed her coat sleeve into her mouth and tears ran down her face. Not even violent punches from the others stifled her laughter.

144

"That was a beautiful story and you ruined it!" Lilian told her as soon as the lights went on.

Some of the audience felt the same way, berating her on the way out.

"You destroyed that picture!"

"Young ones these days don't know how to behave!"

"You lot should've been thrown out!"

This fuelled her friends' indignation. Outside the cinema, Catherine was about to tell Rosie just what she thought of her daft behaviour when Lilian swayed and gripped her arm. "It was too hot in there," she said. "I'll be fine in a minute." But she wasn't.

By the time they got her home, her face was white and she had to be helped up the stairs.

A grim-faced Mrs Hennessey opened the door. "I knew this would happen. You two had better come in."

They helped Lilian across to the old armchair and took off her coat and boots. Mrs Hennessey poured water into a basin and rinsing out a cloth she wiped the beads of sweat from Lilian's face. Soon her daughter's eyes closed and she was breathing deeply.

"I'm sorry," Catherine said. "She looked so well this morning and she was dying to get out."

"She has no patience! Oh, it's all right, don't look so downhearted. I've seen her like this before. She can never wait till she's completely better. Now she'll have to rest for another week, but she'll be fine then."

Rosie's heart lifted. Her plan had worked. "Will she be able to go to Croke Park then?"

"Not unless she wants to go to her own funeral."

"Great!" She caught the others, startled faces. "I mean, it's great she won't take too long to get better."

She saw Lilian's eyes open and went beetroot, realising too late the girl had not been asleep.

145

"You're glad," Lilian said. "You're glad I can't go to that match. I can see it in your face." She closed her eyes again. "You asked me out today because you hoped I'd get sick again, not because you wanted us to be friends."

Unable to explain, Rosie said nothing. She had never felt so mean.

"I was right not to like you. You're sly and you're dangerous and you hate me."

There was silence in the room. Rosie could not bear to look at anyone. She knew they were waiting for her to say something, but she could not. Eventually Catherine took the lead. "I think we'd better go, Mrs Hennessey, and leave Lilian to get some rest."

Lilian did not open her eyes again. Rosie wished the ground would swallow her. She had ruined the day for everyone.

Chapter 13

"SHE ISN'T right, is she?" Catherine asked when they were back in their own room. "You're not trying to spoil things for her?"

"I am not. I wouldn't want anything bad to happen to her. She's wrong about my hating her. Totally wrong!"

Looking at Rosie's strained face and clenched hands, Catherine was almost convinced. "It's just that you sounded glad when her mother said she couldn't go to the match."

"I can't help how I sounded. But I would never do anything to hurt Lilian. It'd be like hurting myself." Rosie bit her lip, aware she had said too much.

But Catherine was nodding. "I believe you. Don't worry any more. Lilian will feel differently when she's well."

At once Rosie felt better. At least Catherine still thought well of her. "It was a really good day until the end," she said. "It's a pity William had to work. He could have come with us. I like him. He's nice."

"He's smashing!" Catherine agreed. "I don't know what me and Mother would've done without him."

"How did you meet him?"

"I met him in the Gresham a few weeks after Father

147

left. We'd no money and Mother was sick. I couldn't get a job, even from Mr Weinberger. He had too much scrap and no statues to sell. Anyway, he wouldn't let me tug on my own. The neighbours had no work either and were short themselves. I couldn't ask them for any more. I thought we were going to starve." She paused, her eyes sombre with the memory.

"Anyway, I thought there might be some scraps in the bins at the back of the hotel. There weren't. But there was a lovely smell of fresh-baked bread coming from the kitchens. I couldn't stand it. I sneaked in. The place was empty. On the table was a batch of hot crusty loaves. Just as I robbed two, William came in the door. I thought I was a goner. I couldn't move with the fright. Then he said 'If you're taking those you'd better skedaddle before anyone else sees you.' I was flying out the door when he shouts, 'I'm William Scott. What's your name?' I didn't tell him."

"Why not?"

"I thought he was trying to trap me. But when I told Mother, she said he was a kind boy and could've lost his job if anyone had seen what happened. So I went back and waited till I saw him through the kitchen window. Then I went in and told him my name. We've been friends ever since. When there's no food, I ask William and he always finds us something."

"What about Mr Callaghan? Does he know?"

"He does. But he thinks the world of William. And he says a lot of the food goes to waste anyway and we only get what'd be thrown out." She giggled. "If he's there when William is giving me leftovers, he always makes the same little speech. Word for word. 'When Ireland is free of the British,' he says, 'there will be no starving poor. We shall sup at the well of plenty. We shall be masters of our own destiny.' He's a bit daft, but nice all the same."

"As nice as William?"

"No. William is the best. He'd give you his last tanner. And he's a laugh. One day the two of us are going to Australia and we'll travel around the whole country having adventures. But don't say a word to Mother. She'd only start fretting again." She smiled. "You should come with me and William to the match on Sunday. Then you can get to know him better."

Rosie shivered. Events were falling too easily into place.

It was two am before William finished polishing the last pair of boots that Friday night. He could not stop thinking about the previous afternoon.

He would never forget his feeling of dread on entering the kitchen. Catherine was white and strained, waiting for some horror to unfold. And Rosie looked ready to crumple. For a split second he was sure Foley intended to kill Brown. He had never seen such anger. Immediately he'd thought – if Foley does this, he'll ruin everything.

He'd imagined the relentless investigation that would have followed. They would have been lifted for interrogation. The Tans would have beaten the truth out of them about everything and then they'd have taken their revenge for Brown. He shivered. Catherine was his best friend. They had made great plans for the years ahead. Yesterday he had seen how fragile the future could be.

"You look tired, William," Mr Callaghan had arrived to inspect his work. He held up a gleaming boot. "You've done a perfect job, lad." William's smile was preoccupied.

"You showed a steady nerve yesterday," Mr Callaghan said.

"You mean I did nothing . . ."

"Exactly. You stayed calm. And afterwards you went on with your work without complaint. I admire you, lad. You'll go far. With my help and training you might even take over from me one day. Head porter! Not bad for a boy from an orphanage, eh?"

"It's not what I want – though I'm very grateful." He was definite and Mr Callaghan, who had worked in the Gresham since he was William's age, was a little hurt.

"Some would think you were very lucky to be given the chance, William. What would you like to do that's so much better?"

"I'd like to travel the world, Mr Callaghan. Go to China and Peru and the South Sea islands."

"That's the stuff of dreams, lad. Better to stay here and make solid progress."

But William was determined. "I have it all planned. I'll get a job as cabin boy, maybe on an ocean liner. That way I'll see the world. And I'll work really hard so people will give me plenty of tips and I'll be able to save."

Mr Callaghan shook his head. "Pipe dreams! How could you get a job on a liner?"

"My uncle from Inchicore is in the Merchant Navy. He knows people. He could get me a job in the morning, except – " he stopped.

"Except what?"

"I'd like to make sure Catherine and her mother are all right. They need my help until Mr Dalton comes home."

"And won't you mind leaving her behind when you're a sailor?"

"It won't be forever. When I've made enough money, I'm going to settle in Australia. Land is cheap there and I'm going to build a small hotel in one of the cities. Then I'll build another one and another. Catherine says she'll come out and help me run them. There are so many people emigrating to Australia, Mr Callaghan. I've read all about it. They'll need good lodgings while they decide where to live and that's how we'll make our fortune."

Mr Callaghan was at a loss for words. "You never said any of this before, lad." William shrugged. The plan had been his and Catherine's secret. Something for her to dream about when times were bad. He wasn't quite sure why he'd said anything now, except that talking about it gave him back his belief in the future. That belief had nearly been shattered when he'd thought Foley was going to kill the Tan.

"So," Mr Callaghan surmised, "You and Catherine will become rich Australians and we'll never see you again."

But once more William took him by surprise. "Yes, you will. When we've made our fortune, Catherine and I will sell the business. We're going to travel around the continent and explore the wilderness. It will be a great adventure. Then we'll come home."

What a wonderful dream, Mr Callaghan thought. It just might come true. The boy had the brains and determination to achieve anything. And young Catherine was his equal.

What was to stop them conquering the future?

William was about to get ready for bed in his small room next to the alcove when he heard the Crossleys. One after another they screeched to a halt outside the hotel. He listened to the pounding boots and the shouting. There must be dozens of them, he thought. He crept along the dark corridor to the door at the main lobby.

The Tans had swarmed upstairs and guests were being ordered out of their rooms. Through a chink in the doorway he watched them come downstairs in dressing-gowns, grumbling at the inconvenience. Overhead a search was under way. Drawers were pulled open and emptied on to the floor. Doors were slammed and luggage tumbled out of presses.

What were they looking for? Signs of Foley? If so, they were a bit late. Anyway, William would have staked his life that Brown had been too terrified to report what had happened yesterday afternoon. So why were they here?

All of the guests were now in the lobby. The officer in charge addressed them. His tone was civil. "Ladies and gentlemen, I must apologise for the inconvenience. We have information which leads us to believe that documents and weapons for use against His Majesty's government have been hidden in the hotel. I hope therefore, you will appreciate our reasons for this search."

To judge from the groans of some of the guests, his hopes were misplaced. One man was louder than the rest. "The only reason is malice, sir! This search could just as easily be carried out in daylight. You are intent on disturbing our rest for some sport of your own!"

Another voice seconded him. "Hear, hear! Abominable behaviour and bad manners, sir! Not to be tolerated by law-abiding citizens."

With a shock William recognised both speakers. They were McCormack and Wilde, the men he had traced for Foley. Somehow he'd have thought Foley's enemies would've been on the side of the Tans.

The officer's voice was icy. "Is there anyone else who wishes to make a complaint?" His eyes swept the room. Silence answered him. He turned to the two men. "Follow me, please. I think a lesson in co-operation is required."

There was an audible intake of breath from the guests. The two men shrank with fear. William thought they were about to be escorted to the Crossleys. Instead the officer moved in his direction. Startled, he stepped back into the shadows and hurried back down the corridor into his room where he slipped under the bed.

"There's no one in here. We're safe enough in this room, gentlemen." The three stepped inside.

"Naturally the raid is a mock-up. There was no other way to contact you without arousing suspicion." The officer's tone was friendly and the others had dropped all pretence of fear. "Well, hurry up, man. Presumably you're here to give us information. What is it?"

"My orders are to tell you the apostles are on to something. You must strike at them, take them by surprise. Tuesday is the earliest we can mobilise. You'll be given the exact details on Monday night."

"Have we found the bank accounts yet? If not, this whole project is futile."

"Stop worrying. On Tuesday we'll have access to the money. Now I'd better take you back to the lobby. Don't forget to play your part in there. Look terrorised."

They laughed, relaxed now their minds were set at ease. William heard the officer shout as they moved down the corridor, "Never question one of His Majesty's auxiliaries again!" The tone was harsh and the mumbled response of the two men suitably cowed.

William crawled out from his hiding-place and sat on the edge of his bed, thinking. Outside he could the Crossleys rev up and move away.

Hugh Callaghan came in. "Are you all right, lad? Did they disturb you?" William told him what he'd overheard.

"No need to worry. They're the ones who'll be taken by surprise. Remember Foley and the apostles will make their move on Sunday, two days ahead of those boyos."

"Who exactly *are* the apostles, Mr Callaghan?"

The head porter drew the chair up opposite William and sat down. "Twelve very daring young men, hand-picked by Michael Collins. Not one of them is much more than twenty and all of them are willing to risk their lives against the enemy."

"What do they do?"

"They're not going to tell us that, lad. Their work has to be secret. I think they spy on British agents, and find out what they're up to so they can stop them. That's what I think, but I'm not sure. Foley is one of them. They want to free Ireland and they need all the help they can get from the likes of us."

William had one more question. "What do you think they'll do on Sunday?"

"I don't know. But whatever it is, it will be very smart. It'll sweep the ground from under the British. They've no hope of getting their dirty hands on Collins's money. He'll keep it safe for the cause."

Chapter 14

NEXT MORNING, Mr Callaghan gave William an hour off to call on the girls. The boy wanted to make sure they were all right after that business with Brown, particularly Catherine. He also wanted to tell them about the raid. Mr Callaghan warned him, "Don't say anything about the apostles. They operate in secret. I shouldn't have told you Foley was one of them. But I trust you to say nothing. Anyway, from what you tell me, young Catherine has enough worries."

So, in William's edited version of events, he never mentioned that Foley was one of that select band of patriots working with Michael Collins. If Rosie had known, it might have made all the difference. She might have remembered her gran's account of Bloody Sunday. She might have tried to change events.

Instead she was relieved to know that Foley had been telling the truth. "So it was about money. McClean and the others are trying to cheat him," she mused, trying to tie up the loose ends that would make Foley the hero she wanted him to be.

"If he's honest why is he friendly with that bank robber – Clancy? Why was I given a gun and money to pass on?"

Catherine gave her the answer. "Foley didn't know

about the robbery. He sent us around to Clancy to take a message. It wasn't his fault Clancy involved us."

"Why did he take the gun and the money then, if he'd nothing to do with the robbery?"

"Because he didn't want you to be caught with them." William was prompt and decisive. "And he had to help out his friend."

Rosie was still not satisfied. "A bank robber is a strange friend for an honest man."

"Well, he *was* very angry with Clancy," Catherine said, "so I don't suppose he's a friend any more. Anyway, how can you still not trust Foley? He saved your life, Rosie!"

None of the three of them wanted Foley to be a villain. They had run his messages, taken his money, witnessed his bravery. He couldn't be bad!

William got up to go. "I don't finish work tomorrow until after lunch. So I'll meet you for the match outside the gates on Jones Road. Afterwards I'm going to visit my uncle in Inchicore. I got a message this morning to say his ship is in."

From his pocket he took two tickets. "Here. Better take these. If I'm delayed go ahead and I'll see you inside. You'd best have Lilian's ticket, Rosie."

Catherine looked at the tickets and gasped. "William! These cost two shillings!"

He grinned sheepishly. "They're a present. I got a lot of money in tips this week."

Delighted, she hugged him. "These are the berries!"

Suddenly William shivered. "This room is very cold."

The girls were startled. They had lit the fire early and now it was blazing. Even Rosie, used to central heating, thought the room was cosy. "You must be getting the flu," she told William.

"No. I'm warm again now."

Then Catherine said carelessly, "Someone walking over your grave. At least that's what Mother says if she suddenly shivers."

She and William laughed, but Rosie's heart stopped, thinking that tomorrow after the match, the other two would not be so light-hearted about death. The prospect of Croke Park, now only a day away, filled her with dismay. How was she to endure it, knowing what would happen? She must concentrate on her reason for being here, otherwise she might lose her courage and stay away from the match.

After all, she thought, Gran is safe because she can't go. I just have to find out what happens to Catherine. If I keep my nerve I can do that. It can't be bad or it would have been in the papers and Gran said there was nothing.

Much happier now, she vowed "All I have to do is stick close to Catherine. I won't let her out of my sight."

They spent their day sitting by the fire, talking. Knowing her time with Catherine was running out, Rosie was conscious of trying to store away these hours in her memory. She wanted to recall everything about Catherine, even the silly joke she told:

Catherine: What do you get hanging from an apple tree?

Rosie: Apples.

Catherine: No, sore arms!

Late in the afternoon, Mrs Hennessey knocked on their door and entered.

"If you're not off gallivanting, maybe you'd have a bit of tea with us?" She saw Rosie's delight and smiled, "Lilian will be glad to see you. She's feeling much better. Don't worry, she won't bite you! She'd just like a bit of company her own age."

Catherine nodded and said, "We were going to call in before but didn't want to disturb her. Especially if she was still upset at Rosie."

"Not at all. I told her there was no point blaming others for her own foolhardy ways. She took the decision to go out before she was better and she can't blame Rosie for that. All the same, she'd like to see her pals. Come down in about half an hour. I'll have a nice tea for you – Mr H has been working all week, so it's herrings and a bit of tripe as a treat!"

Tripe! The lining of a sheep's stomach! Rosie felt sick, but Catherine was positively drooling.

When they went down some time later, Mrs Hennessey was in the middle of a tirade.

"If one of you boys touches anything on that table again, you'll be bound and gagged."

The three boys reminded Rosie of Gran's photo, only now they were dressed in ragged jumpers and trousers that looked like hand-me-downs. And instead of polite expressions for the camera, they were glaring mutinously at their mother. The eldest, Joseph, was rubbing his ear.

"We're starving. It's not fair. We haven't eaten for hours."

Hands on hips, their mother glared back. "You're like magicians, you three. Food disappears when you're around. Nobody ever sees it go and not one of you knows who took it. I put a plate of bread down on that table three minutes ago and what happened? For one instant I turned my back and now there's only crumbs left! Well, it's not to happen again, do you hear!" She leaned towards them and they backed away hastily. "That's it. Sit down against the wall and don't move till I say your tea is ready."

Sulkily, they did as they were told. Lilian, who was helping to set the table, beamed at the girls and Rosie at once felt happier.

Chunks of fresh bread and a dish of smoked herrings were put on the table. Mr Hennessey came in and nodded at the girls. Seeing his three sons sitting at the wall he grinned, "The raiding party's been caught again has it?"

They took this as a signal to rise but their mother stopped them. "You three! Stay where you are until I've shared out the food, otherwise not even your father will get any."

She set a bowl of tripe in each place. When she poured the tea she let everyone sit down, the boys on upturned boxes, Lilian in the armchair, parents and visitors on rickety chairs. Managing to eat and at the same time keep their balance was quite a feat.

Rosie could not bear to touch the tripe. It looked like a white fat sponge with large holes and it was floating in yellowish greasy liquid. She thought of a sheep's stomach and everything that went into it – grass, nettles, weeds . . . slimy worms. Her own stomach heaved.

Joseph dropped a piece of bread and as Mrs Hennessey bent to retrieve it, he swopped his already empty dish for Rosie's full one. She smiled gratefully.

She was not too fond of herring, either, but in spite of her protests Mrs Hennessey insisted on placing one in her empty tripe bowl. "Sure you must be starving, child. You ate that tripe as fast as one of my own!"

Rosie made encouraging signs at Joseph, but when he dropped the bread again his mother gave him a smack on the head. "We don't have so much food that you can be flinging it on the floor, Joseph!" And while he and Mrs Hennessey glared at each other it was Jamesie this time who made the successful snatch.

"My God, you'll give yourself terrible stomach pains, bolting your food like that! You didn't even leave the bones." Mrs Hennessey studied Rosie's empty dish in bewilderment, but her expression was mild compared to Joseph's when he realised the coveted fish was gone.

All this time Mr H concentrated on his food, paying no attention to the shenanigans at the table.

Afterwards, when they were sitting around the fire, Mrs Hennessey turned to Rosie. "Is your memory any better, love?"

"It's just the same as Monday," she said and her great-grandmother sighed.

"So you really don't remember anything about the past?" Catherine said.

"You mean like last year? 1919? No, I'm afraid not."

"I wonder where you came from," Catherine went on. "You could have a family somewhere worried sick about you!"

Mrs Hennessey put a comforting hand on Rosie's shoulder. "When Mrs Dalton come home from hospital and Dr Sullivan calls to see her, you tell him about your memory. Maybe he can help."

Rosie nodded and, to reassure her, said, "I might not know about the past but I reckon I know about the future." Seeing Lilian's swift frown she said hastily," I mean I know what I'd like to do when I grow up."

"And what's that?" her great-grandmother asked.

Rosie wanted to be an engineer, but she knew better than to say so in 1920. Mom had told her that until the seventies girls did not do such jobs as engineering. What about her other ambition? She vaguely

160

remembered the name Amelia Earhart. Was she around yet? She took a chance.

"I'd like to learn to fly."

Silence greeted this. Mrs Hennessey started patting Rosie's shoulder, soothingly. Her great-grandfather puffed on a pipe and gazed into the distance. Lilian stared at her intently. Catherine opened and shut her mouth. Joseph caught his brothers' eyes and sniggered.

Rosie groaned inwardly. She should have known women pilots would be out of the question.

"You can't fly, love," Her great-grandmother told her gently, "only men fly aeroplanes and even then it's against nature."

"Will you three stop laughing!" Lilian turned on her brothers and added defiantly, "I don't see why she shouldn't be what she wants."

Rosie sighed. She'd gone through all this before in 1956. Maybe she should try reason.

"Why can't I be a pilot?" she asked Joseph. He hooted, "Because you're a girl."

"So?"

He stared at her. "So! A dog can't be a cat and a girl can't be a pilot. It's not natural." Everyone nodded in agreement.

But Rosie tried again, "Of course a dog or a cat couldn't be pilots," she said calmly, and waited patiently as her great-uncles exploded with mirth.

"Imagine a cat flying!" Christy was chortling.

"Or a dog in the leather jacket!" Jamesie thought this so funny he doubled up.

"Dogs and cats don't fly," Rosie continued calmly, "because they haven't got the brains. But girls have the brains."

Her great-grandmother sighed, still patting her

161

shoulder, "The sooner you see Dr Sullivan the better," she said. "He might be able to cure you."

Rosie fumed, "Well, there *will* be women pilots and engineers and computer experts and bus drivers and TV announcers."

"If you say so. No need to upset yourself." Mrs Hennessey spoke softly, as if she were trying to comfort someone who was gravely ill. "Just make sure you see the doctor when he comes next week."

"Rambling," she mouthed to her husband, tapping her forehead when she thought Rosie wasn't looking.

"And what's a TV announcer? and a compu – a compu whatever it is, expert?" Lilian's frown was back again and Rosie knew it would be no good to explain.

"Leave the girl alone, she's not well," Mrs Hennessey said. "You tell us, Lilian, what would you like to do when you grow up?"

"Marry," she was prompt, "have a family, live in a nice house. Have plenty of clothes and never be hungry."

Disappointed, Rosie said, "Don't you want to have adventures and a career?"

"*I* want adventures – " Catherine cut in. "I want to travel. I shall go to Australia and explore wild places and have pots of money and be very happy. And when you come to visit, Rosie, I shall have a proper toilet for you. There'll be a sign on the door saying 'Rosie's Lavatory'."

"I'll have three toilets in my house and a huge tin bath," said the eight-year-old Jamesie, "and I'll have a full chocolate cake every day!"

Rosie smiled broadly. She knew Jamesie had gone to Birmingham before he was eighteen and started work as a door-to-door salesman, selling perfume to housewives.

162

Gran had said his good looks and charm had earned him a fortune, not his perfume. He eventually built a factory, made a fortune and left it all to charity.

"You'll be able to have mountains of chocolate cake every day," she mused aloud.

"I'm going to go to America," Christy stated and I'm going to find gold and drive a big motor-car." He would change his mind, Rosie knew. Christy had become a priest, joined the foreign missions and lived most of his life in Africa.

"And what will you do, Joseph?" Mrs Hennessey asked.

"I'd like to be an artist," he said gravely, "and spend my whole life painting in foreign lands."

But Joseph had never left Ireland. He'd married before he was twenty and had a large family, working hard at the building trade all his life. She hadn't even known he *could* paint.

"Do you have any pictures you can show me?" she asked.

"Only pencil drawings," he said, "paint is too dear." From under his mattress he took some pages, carefully protected by brown paper. He passed them to Rosie. "I draw people," he said. She looked at them. A drawing of her great-grandfather raking a few coals in an almost empty hearth, his pipe at the side of his mouth, not a puff of smoke coming from it. Then one of Christy and Jamesie cramming food into their mouths and a clever picture of his mother gazing at a mirror, her face careworn, but her reflection showing a beautiful young girl. Finally there was a portrait of his sister Lilian, her eyes dreamy, at variance with her determined mouth.

Lilian had got what she wanted, Rosie thought. She'd had her family and her nice house. Why should she feel sad about that? The girl who had looted shops and challenged policemen and who thought it was fine to be an engineer, what was sad about her becoming a respectable married woman?

Mrs Hennessey snatched the picture from Rosie. "Why, she looks just like you!" They crowded round the drawing, then stared at Rosie who made faces and beamed, to look as unlike her grandmother as possible.

Lilian was indignant. "Look at her hair, she doesn't look a bit like me!"

"You're smaller and thinner," Catherine agreed.

"Rosie looks like a convict," Jamesie said, not very diplomatically.

"Her expression's not a bit like Lilian's," Mr Hennessey said, looking at Rosie's contortions in consternation.

Mrs Hennessey sighed. You're right. It must be a trick of the light."

Satisfied, Rosie smiled normally, till she noticed Joseph studying her. He nodded to himself, then said, "I'd like to draw your picture, Rosie, if you don't mind. Oh, I don't want you posing, I'd prefer to do it from memory." Rosie nodded agreement. She would be long gone by the time he had drawn her. It wouldn't really matter if she looked like Gran.

When they left, Lilian came out on to the landing with them. She put her hand on Rosie's arm. "I'm sorry I was so bad-tempered the other day. It's my own fault I can't go to Croke Park, not yours."

"That's all right," Rosie blushed. She had wanted Lilian to have a relapse, but only so she'd be safe. Nevertheless she felt mean.

"It'd be nice if we could be friends and start again," Lilian said.

Carefully Rosie chose her words, "In the future," she said, "I bet we'll get on really well!"

Chapter 15

"TROUBLED TIMES, Rosie." Gran's voice was sorrowful. "So much violence. So many people killed."

McClean's face, tense and white, swam into view. Foley appeared, bright-eyed and smiling, "The future is ours, Rosie." Then McLean disappeared.

"A great time!" Foley boomed. "Time for another joke. What do you get from hanging? A sore neck, that's what. Oh a great time for a football match! Here's another one. When is a match not a match? You know the answer to that one, Rosie!" He guffawed, his gleaming teeth growing bigger until he was all teeth and no face. Then the teeth cackled at her and disappeared.

She heard the sound of gunfire and yelling crowds. People surged past her. She looked around in panic. Where was Catherine? She could not find her, after coming all this way. Her tears flowed for Gran's lost friend. Hopelessly she called, "Catherine! Where are you? Please, please! Where are you?"

"I'm here, you ninny! Wake up, Rosie. Will you stop wailing and wake up!" Catherine shook her.

Rosie jumped and sat up at once knocking her friend over. Wide-eyed and heaving for breath, she took in the familiar contours of the room. Rubbing her eyes, she was surprised to find her face wet.

"You were bawling," Catherine said. "I thought you were dying. And you were roaring my name."

"I had a nightmare," Rosie said, remembering it vividly.

"Oh, I'd never have guessed." Catherine tried to cheer her up. "Usually when people bawl and roar in their sleep it's because they've never been so happy and – "

"Foley!" Rosie said. "He was with McLean. Then he said the future belonged to us and McClean disappeared. What does it mean, Catherine?"

"It means nothing! You were having a nightmare, that's all."

"Foley was horrible, Catherine. He went on and on about the match tomorrow."

Her friend sighed, "What exactly did he say?"

"He asked me when was a match not a match . . ." Even as she spoke Rosie knew it sounded ridiculous.

"I see . . . and that's why you were screaming your head off, was it?"

"Part of the reason, yes."

"Look, Rosie, you had a nightmare. It's not real. You probably ate too much herring. Go back to sleep. You'll feel much better in the morning."

Rosie did not answer. She wanted to convince her friend that Foley was up to some villainy, but she knew it was pointless to try. Catherine had never listened to her doubts about him.

So what should she do?

She would tell William and ask his advice. She remembered his face when he'd seen Foley attack the Tan soldier. He did not believe Foley was a saint. She would tell him about the match too. She would see what he thought of her fears. And if she was wrong and the nightmare was not connected to reality, William might help her see that. His shift started at eight am. She would call on him then.

But she did not wake up till much later. Catherine was still fast asleep. Rosie dressed silently and crept out of the room. She'd be back before her friend woke up. The church bells were ringing out as she raced down the street, pausing only to ask the time.

"Just after a quarter to nine," a man said. "Plenty of time if you're going to Mass."

It'd be nice, she thought wistfully, just to be on her way to Mass. A church would be so peaceful compared to what lay ahead.

At least William would be at work now, she reckoned, her feet running faster than they'd ever done. Coming down the hill to Sackville Street, she got a stitch in her side and had to stop, gasping for breath. Hands holding her ribs, she stumbled on, unable to run any more. About to turn down North Earl Street for the lane behind the hotel, she paused.

Now the hour bells were ringing. Nine o'clock.

Sackville Street was silent. A man with a newspaper stood in front of the Gresham. By the kerb was a Daimler, engine rumbling. Perhaps it was that which caught her attention. Or maybe it was the man with the paper, who constantly looked around, while he flicked through the pages, reading nothing.

Rosie approached the car, and peered in. Not Foley, anyway. The driver turned and saw her. He jumped, his face rigid with shock. "Go away," he hissed. "Get out of here! Quick!"

167

The man with the newspaper watched her anxiously. At the same time he kept an eye on the street.

Rosie looked at the front door of the hotel, back to the driver and down the street. It was a glorious day. But the stillness was dreadful. It was as if the world were holding its breath, waiting for some catastrophe.

The man at the door folded his paper and gave a piercing whistle.

Suddenly there was mayhem. The doors of the Gresham burst open and a group of young men rushed out, overcoats flying, firing guns in the air. They scattered in all directions, some on foot, one on a bike, two of them coming for the car.

She could not move and the first man pushed her aside, wrenching open the back door. She stumbled and fell. Then she saw his companion. Foley. He stopped, reached down and helped her to her feet.

"Get in! Don't mind the kid! Come on!" The driver was yelling.

Foley tried to smile, not managing at all, and for the life of her Rosie could not smile back. Briefly he put a hand on her shoulder. Then he was into the car and it screeched off. For a long moment the street returned to silence.

Rosie's head whirled, trying to make some sense of what she'd seen.

Next minute the head porter, Hugh Callaghan, was beside her, helping her through the front door of the hotel.

Inside, the lobby was crowded with people, some of them half-dressed, some still in dressing-gowns, all of them, staff and guests, totally silent, faces shocked.

"Down here, Rosie." Mr Callaghan led her along the corridor to William's room. The boy was there, silent, sitting on the side of the bed, staring at the floor. He did not look up when they came in.

"What happened?" Rosie whispered

Hugh Callaghan swallowed, unable to answer.

"William, what happened? Tell me! I saw Foley and the other men running out firing their guns. What did they do?"

"They killed Wilde and McCormack," William's voice was flat.

Rosie could not breathe. She gazed anxiously at William's face as if she might find the answer there. Her heart stopped with dread and she felt a huge sense of loss. She tried to understand. It was as if Foley had died, not the two strangers.

"Believe me, I did not know what they intended," Hugh Callaghan's voice was anguished. "When I came into the kitchens this morning, they were waiting. Foley told me – ordered me – to take them to Mr Wilde's room. Number 14. There was no arguing. They were deadly serious.

"'Knock on the door', Foley said when we got there. No one else said anything. They were standing behind me.

"'Who's there?' Wilde shouted. Foley prodded me. I had trouble answering, but Wilde mustn't have noticed, because he opened the door and smiled at me . . . Then he saw the others. I thought he was going to fall, he looked so sick.

"'It's all right Sir,' I said. Such stupid, stupid words. I think I was trying to make him feel better. Part of my job.

"Foley pushed me out of the way and one of his men fired three times at point-blank range. Wilde just crumpled. There wasn't that much blood, just a few spots on the carpet . . . I wondered if the stain would be hard to get out . . ."

He stopped a moment, then went on savagely, "You'd think, wouldn't you, that with a man dying in front of you, you'd have more on your mind than stains on the carpet. But then, I'm the perfect servant. Born with my cap in hand. Dear God! I couldn't refuse an order, even from a young fellow like Foley."

He leaned against the wall and wiped his brow, eyes full of grief. He went on, "Then Foley ordered me to take them to Captain McCormack's room. Number 24. But I couldn't move. My eyes were fixed on Wilde. He was curled up like a baby in the doorway. The shots must've been heard along the corridor, but no one looked out.

"Foley knew where the room was, anyway, and led the way, pushing me along with them. This time I couldn't say a word and McCormack wouldn't open the door. They hammered on it. Then Foley fired at the keyhole and a few of them charged and it gave way. McCormack was halfway out of his bed. He should have been out the window. I don't know why he was so slow. They pumped five bullets into him. This time there was blood everywhere. They ran past me and down the stairs. Everyone in the hotel heard them. People crowded on to the landing, but that was when they were gone. No one tried to stop them."

Stillness enveloped them. William sitting on the bed, Hugh Callaghan leaning against the wall, Rosie standing in the centre of the room, her eyes fixed on some invisible distance.

Outside, the sounds of life began again. Doors opened and shut. Someone shouted, "Mr Callaghan! Mr

Callaghan! The police are here." They heard footsteps, voices. Hugh Callaghan at last began to move.

"I'd better go back," he said. "They'll want me to help with their enquiries." In a trance they watched him go. In a trance they followed him.

The lobby was full of men in uniforms, officers, Tans, police.

"Everyone must go to their rooms at once," an officer addressed the milling crowd. "Stay there until further notice. Each person in this hotel will be questioned." The police shepherded the guests away and very soon there was no one left except the hotel staff, the military and Rosie.

The officer snapped orders now. "No one is to enter this hotel or to leave it. I want three soldiers on every exit."

Still bemused, it took time to dawn on Rosie that the man giving the orders was the captain who'd led the raid on the tenement. Too busy, he had not yet noticed her. But someone else had.

She saw Corporal Brown staring at her. His eyes narrowed. Then he made up his mind. "That kid," he shouted, "she was the one who took the gun from the bank robber." Now the captain's attention was caught and he recognised her. "Grab that urchin!" he yelled.

Hugh Callaghan and William stepped in front of her and William whispered – "go, Rosie, run!" She turned and hared down the corridor into William's room and, standing on a box, opened a window and levered herself into the lane.

Already there were voices behind her, "Stop or I'll fire!"

"Get back here!"

But the window was too small to allow a man

through, and incredibly, there was no one guarding the lane. She was safe for the moment.

There was no time to lose. They knew where she lived and would go there. She had to warn Catherine. Fervently she hoped they would be delayed in the hotel a bit longer. William and Mr Callaghan would try to stall them.

Bursting into the tenement room she saw Catherine at the table and hauled her to her feet. "Get out!" she yelled. "Come on, the Tans are after us." Catherine asked no questions. She followed Rosie in a headlong flight from the tenement.

At the corner Rosie snapped, "Where can we go?" She was desperate.

Catherine thought quickly. "Where we were the other day, beside the river. I know a watchman's hut that's not being used." They rushed towards the Liffey, using whatever alleyways and back streets they could. They heard ambulances and Crossleys in the distance and, once, the sound of gunfire.

Way down the North Wall Catherine stopped at the shed. "The lock doesn't work properly," she said, deftly picking it with a hairpin until the door pushed in easily.

Inside Rosie told her what happened and Catherine was aghast. "Foley?" she gasped, "Foley?" She closed her eyes.

"I liked him," Rosie said. "I never thought he'd kill anyone. The worst I thought he'd do was smash someone with his fist, like he wanted to do to Brown."

"He was so generous," Catherine said, "and he saved your life." They were silent, neither of them realising they had spoken of Foley in the past tense, as if he no longer existed.

There was something else on Rosie's mind, and

eventually she said, "We really shouldn't go to the match today."

Catherine looked weary. "We have to go to the match. William will be waiting for us. If we don't turn up, he'll think the Tans got us. We must let him know we're safe."

"But the Tans won't let him out of the hotel. They're going to question everyone. It'll take all day."

"You don't know William. He'll want to know what happened to us. One way or another he'll get out of that hotel."

A couple of hours before the match was due to start, they made their way through the streets towards Jones's Road and Croke Park.

The Tans were everywhere, questioning people, raiding houses, tearing around in their Crossleys. Avoiding them made the girls' progress slow.

It dawned on them that in spite of the Tans there were an awful lot of civilians on the streets, mostly in small nervous groups, standing in doorways or at corners. There was an air of dread about them, of barely suppressed excitement.

"Why do you think so many people are out?" Rosie wondered. "Usually they disappear when the Tans are around."

"Let's ask someone," Catherine said.

She caught the eye of a girl standing with some women and signalled to her. The girl came over willingly, eyes gleaming. "Isn't it shocking?" she breathed.

"Do you mean what happened in the Gresham?" Rosie said.

"Not just the Gresham. Did you not hear?" She paused, milking the moment of its drama.

"Hear what? Tell us. Please."

"Fancy you not hearing," she said. "Where were you – on another planet?"

She was taking a keen enjoyment in prolonging the suspense. Rosie felt like strangling her. Instead she shrugged, "Oh well, if you're not going to tell us – " and they made to move off.

"British agents were murdered!" The girl spoke quickly, and to her satisfaction the girls stopped in their tracks.

"All over the city," the words tumbled out now. "Collins's men did it. At nine o'clock this morning, they turned up in different places and – bang!" She raised an imaginary gun and fired, "They blasted them."

"Where did it happen?" Rosie was hysterical. She gripped the girl and stuttered the question. "What parts of the city?"

"Hey! Steady on. That's my arm you're breaking!" The girl smiled, unable to hide her satisfaction at the impact of her words. "Collins' squads turned up all over the south side. Baggot Street, Mount Street, Morehampton Road, Pembroke Street and other places. Fourteen men were killed. All of them shot at nine o'clock exactly!"

"Morehampton Road!" They moved back from the girl, terror gripping them. Rosie's heart plummeted.

"Yes. Three men."

"How do you know all this?" Catherine could barely ask the question.

"Everyone knows it. Everybody told everybody else. You two must be the last to hear." Looking at their sickened faces, she said, "It's awful, isn't it? For the poor young fellow in Morehampton Road, I mean. He opened the door to the squad. They killed his father in front of him." Recounting this detail, her voice lost some of its relish. "You two look very pale," she said, "Are you all right?"

They nodded. She had loved telling them the bad news and they could no longer bear her. Quickly they moved away.

Silently they made for the park in Mountjoy Square. It was empty and they sat in the sunlight, grieving.

"Tommy Herbert opened the door," Rosie said. She thought of the eager boy who had given them sixpence for a go in the basket car. He had seen his father and his father's friends shot down. Then an image of McClean reading M's letter came unbidden. Whoever M was, she had loved the captain and praised his bravery. Now she would never see him alive again.

She bowed her head, "My dream wasn't clear enough. I dreamed Foley was laughing and McLean looked white as a sheet, then disappeared. But I didn't understand any of it."

Catherine's arm was around her shoulder. "Don't cry, Rosie. Think of something good. We're safe and so is William."

"We shouldn't go to the match," Rosie said. "The Tans are going to turn up. People will get killed there."

Catherine looked frightened. "How can you know this? Was it your dream?" She stopped short, struck by a dreadful idea. "You didn't," she swallowed, "you didn't see William and me in your dream, did you? You didn't dream that we were killed?"

"No," Rosie said, remembering what Gran had told her. "You won't be killed, though I don't know exactly what will happen. I only know the match is dangerous."

Catherine linked her friend's arm. "We'll tell William, though I don't think he'll believe in your dream. Anyway, if there wasn't anything bad in it for us, we don't have to worry about getting killed. Nothing will happen to us. We have so many plans for the future, me and William. I don't believe anything could go wrong. It wouldn't be fair."

McClean must have had plans too, Rosie thought. That hadn't stopped him dying.

Chapter 16

IT WAS nearly two o'clock when they got to Croke Park. The afternoon was beautiful, crisp and cold. Crowds streamed towards the gates. The rumours, rife among them, did not affect their pleasure at the prospect of the game. Idly Rosie listened to the chatter.

"Nothing to do with us."

"We can't change anything. Might as well enjoy ourselves."

"Live by the gun, die by the gun, that's what I say."

"Tipperary deserve to win. By God, they do!"

"Not at all, Dublin is the best team in the country."

Rosie watched the crowd. Fathers and small sons. Teenage boys. Some women and girls. She thought of warning them and quickly decided against it. Catherine hadn't believed her for ages, so why would complete strangers? They'd probably call an ambulance to take her away. None of them would see any connection between a friendly football match and what had happened that morning.

Her attention was caught by two young men nearby. They wore the soft hats and long overcoats she had come to associate with Foley and his kind. She strained to listen.

"Did you hear Clancy was lifted?" The male voice was urgent.

"How was he? He was told to scarper!"

"Aye. But he went back to his shop and the Tans were waiting for him."

The other man brooded a moment and said, "There's no safety in the old haunts. Clancy is a fool. Right now, Croke Park is the only place to be, lost in the crowd."

Again, Rosie had an overwhelming urge to tell them not to go in, but by the time she moved towards them, they had gone through the turnstile and vanished.

"It's nearly time and we still haven't seen William." Catherine came across from the entrance she'd been watching.

"He mustn't have been able to get away from the hotel," Rosie said, relieved. Now they could leave.

"Don't be silly. I told you. William wouldn't miss this match. And he'd want to know that we were all right."

"He was very upset this morning."

"All the more reason for him to go to the match, then. He'd need cheering up. No, he must have gone in. He's always at the same part of the grounds. It shouldn't be too hard to find him."

It wasn't. They made for the Jones Road side of the pitch. The players were already on the field and the last stragglers were finding a place to watch.

"There he is!" Catherine said.

Rosie began to signal at William to come down to them, but he wasn't looking, and someone asked her to stay quiet. The game was starting. The players' long shorts somehow looked too big for them and the game didn't seem as fast as Rosie remembered it, but otherwise it was played much the same as over three-quarters of a century later, when her dad watched it on telly.

She checked on William. This time he saw her and raised a hand, smiling down at her. He no longer looked overwrought, just a little pale. She beckoned but he was wedged in by the crowd and shook his head.

"He can't move," she told Catherine. "What should we do?"

"Nothing. We can't move either."

Rosie looked around her. There were thousands of people on all sides. Every available space was packed and there was no way to get out without causing a disturbance.

She turned to watch the pitch, paying little attention to the game.

The crowds cheered as the players ran up and down. A Tip supporter beside her roared at the goalkeeper, "Good on you, Hogan! That's the boyo!" as a goal was saved. Whenever the action on the field drew near the posts, the excitement intensified and the roars were deafening.

All the time Rosie waited, watching the field but seeing little beyond a blur of bodies.

Overhead came the noise of an engine. A few spectators were pointing at the sky. She looked up to see a small plane swoop low over the crowd and disappear into the distance.

Then came the rumble she was expecting. Beside her, Catherine caught her breath. "Crossleys!" she said. No one else noticed, intent on cheering their team.

"Go for it, Tip! Beat the Dubs!"

"Up Dublin! Come on, lads!"

Good-natured banter between rival supporters started beside her.

"If those Dubs went any slower they'd be statues!"

"Oh, and I suppose Tip'd run away with the ball – if they could only get hold of it. Butterfingers, the whole lot of them!"

As the rumble grew louder, the girls closed their eyes, nerves tingling. In the animated crowd they were the only ones who were silent and still.

The whistle went for a penalty against Dublin. The spectators roared as a Tip player seized the ball. He was poised for the kick when through the main gateway, armoured cars and lorries drove on to the field, taking up positions at the four corners.

The cheers faded. People looked at each other, uneasily.

"What are they doing here?"

"Do you think they're after someone? Maybe the boyos who did this morning's work?"

"Well, it's certain they're not here to see the Gaelic! Ignorant sods!"

For a moment after the first anxiety, anger took hold. A few people shouted, "Get off the pitch! Let the game go on!" The Tip player unfroze and kicked the ball.

Then the Tans jumped out of the armoured cars and there was total silence. Dropping to one knee, they delayed no longer. Raising their weapons, bayonets already fixed, they began firing.

Stillness erupted into panic. Men lifted their children and pushed at others blocking their way. A mad scramble to escape began. The amiable crowd became a terrified and uncontrollable mob, a force that drove forward, pushing aside human obstacles, trampling on bodies, in a blind surge towards the exit.

Catherine was torn away from Rosie's side. The gunfire was indiscriminate. The man beside Rosie clambered around her, then clutched his throat and dropped without a word. Rosie looked down into his staring eyes and froze.

Everywhere was the sound of terror and pain and relentless gunfire. In the sea of moving bodies, Rosie stood stock-still. Miraculously she was not hurt.

Gradually the power of thought returned.

What about William and Catherine?

At last able to move, she looked around. She saw Catherine immediately, hunkered down beside a small wall while people streamed past her.

"Rosie! Hurry up. Don't stay there. You'll be killed! Hurry up!" Catherine was roaring at her.

William was gone from his position above. Scanning the field, she saw him swept by the crowd towards an exit. With less than twenty yards to go, she reckoned the surge would bring him safely through. His head was turned in her direction and she waved frantically. "We'll be all right," she shouted, though he could not possibly hear in all that noise. Yet she could have sworn he was satisfied. His hand went up in a gesture of recognition and he turned away, focusing his attention on the gate.

"Catherine, Catherine!" she yelled and pushed with all her might over to her friend. Huddled beside her, they watched the scene.

Some supporters at the front, propelled by the masses behind, chose to make their way across the pitch, throwing down hats and ripping off overcoats which hampered their progress. Others had reached the wall at the top of the bank on the opposite side and were hurling themselves over. All the time the Tans were firing. Rosie's gaze was attracted by a boy younger than herself who raced, weaving, across the field. She caught the glint of metal and saw a Tan raise his rifle and take careful aim. The boy stopped in his tracks and fell.

She stood up, terrified, but Catherine pulled her down again. Bowing her head, she tried to close her ears and eyes to the mayhem. Catherine was tugging at her sleeve.

"Where's William? We have to find him."

"I saw him near the farther gate. He must be safe by now."

"Rosie, let's move. We can go down and around this wall, or we can jump over it. Either way we're at an exit. What do you think?"

"Which is the quickest?"

Catherine indicated over the wall. Her friend nodded.

"Wait till I count to three," Catherine said.

Bracing herself Rosie waited, taking a last look at the field. The Tans were streaming across the pitch now. Coats and hats were strewn all over it. A player lay stretched out at the Tipperary end and there were bodies everywhere.

On the far side, at the bottom of the bank, she noticed a small child standing, bewildered. A woman tried to grab his hand but he pulled away and even at that distance Rosie could see he was crying. There was something familiar about him. A man came tumbling down the bank and swooped him up. With a shock she recognised her great-grandfather. The boy was Jamesie. She saw them reach the wall at the top and the tall man push his son across. Joseph and Christy were beside him now and all three clambered after Jamesie.

They were safe.

At last Catherine gave the signal and they flung themselves over the wall. It was only when Rosie was tumbling over that she realised there was at least an eight-foot drop on the other side. They were about to fall on to the crowd rushing out.

"Holy mother of God!" Looking up, a stocky middle-aged man averted tragedy. Pressing close against the wall, he seized both of them as they fell. They bumped and scraped downwards, but he managed to steady them on to their feet and push them safely before him through the exit.

They stayed with him all the way down Jones Road and into Drumcondra.

"Thanks for saving us, Mister," Catherine said as soon as she got the chance.

"Those murdering scum!" he raged. "Slaughtering innocent people. Oh this is the end of them, you mark my words. This time they'll have to go! Filthy butchers!"

"Are you with the IRA?" Rosie asked.

"Who isn't, after today? I saw a young woman lying at the edge of the pitch, beyond help, her clothes mucky from trampling boots, her face – " His fury gave way to incoherent grief. The devil you know . . . there was no call . . . no call at all . . . no matter what Collins . . . innocent people . . ."

They looked at each other, embarrassed as he fought to control his emotions.

"You kids better get on home," he managed at last. "Your mothers'll be fretting. It's dangerous to be on the streets."

He hurried off and waved a hand as they thanked him again.

"What will we do?" Rosie said. "Where can we go?"

"I'll have to let Mother know I'm safe. She's going to find out what happened as soon as the first ambulance arrives at the hospital. She'll be worried sick. And what about William? He'll be anxious too."

"There's nothing he can do," Rosie said. "He couldn't hang around Croke Park waiting for us. The Tans would shoot him. Anyway, I reckon he knows we're safe." She remembered what Gran had told her. "He'll have gone straight to his uncle in Inchicore and won't be back for a week."

"That's right." Catherine was relieved. "He said he'd go after the match – though I don't think he mentioned staying a week. We'll find him later. Right now, I've got to get to the hospital."

Chapter 17

IN HENRY Street they joined what was a procession of walking wounded, making their way to the hospital. Some of them looked quite weak. One man held his left arm gingerly, blood seeping through his fingers. Rosie saw a girl clutching her side, supported by her companion as she limped slowly and painfully towards Jervis Street. There were people with bloodied faces, their eyes dazed. One young man had no coat and was shivering, his shirt front drenched with blood.

The winter sunlight enveloped the silent men and women in a weak yellow glow and the procession moved as in a nightmare.

In Jervis Street hospital staff, normally so strict on visiting, were too busy to notice the girls.

Entering the ward, Catherine gave a cry of joy. "Father!" She rushed down to the smiling man who was seated at her mother's bed. He rose, opened his arms wide and hugged her.

"Thank heavens you are safe," he said. "Your mother told me you'd gone to the match and I was about to go looking for you." He hugged Catherine again, his love and relief obvious.

Mrs Dalton was beaming at them. In spite of the day's tragedy she was happy.

For months she had worried about her husband. Often she and Catherine had faced starvation. Now he was home and her daughter had come back safely from Croke Park, where by all accounts the toll of dead and injured was huge.

She could not hide her joy. "Isn't it wonderful! I never doubted you, Henry, even after all that time not hearing from you."

Her husband was sorrowful. "I didn't write at first, Molly, because I had no good news," he said, "no job and no money. But I knew you'd be worried and asked a fellow who was going home to let you know I was safe and was thinking of you. Last month I heard he took a ship to Lisbon instead. So I wrote then. I had just got a job and there was decent news at last."

"We got no letter," Catherine said.

Mr Dalton sighed. "I heard the mail was being interfered with by the British Intelligence Service. Maybe that's what happened. I don't know. When I got no reply I decided to come over. I arrived home this morning to find neither wife nor daughter. You don't know how disappointed I was. Then I met Dr O'Sullivan coming out of Mrs O'Brien's and he told me you, Molly, were in Jervis Street. The shock I got! I got another one when the Tans arrived as I was coming down the stairs. It was no time to hang around and call on the neighbours. So I came straight over here." He paused, running out of breath.

"We never gave up, Henry," Mrs Dalton assured him and Catherine nodded, "we knew you'd come back."

Her husband patted her shoulder, smiling at her. "Now you're better we can go home. After your convalescence we'll go to Manchester. I've a good job there now and we can start again."

"We can't go home," Catherine said, "not to the tenement. Not yet, anyway."

She told her parents what had happened, with Rosie filling in the gaps. Mrs Dalton's face drained of colour. Mr Dalton sat quite still, frowning with concentration. After a few minutes he said, "If the Tans are after you, we'd better go to England on the first boat. We can't take the risk of going back to the room. So we'll go straight from here, stay overnight in Kingstown and get the mail boat in the morning. What do you say?"

Mrs Dalton looked quite weak. "Not say goodbye to the neighbours?" she said, "They've been so good to us."

"We can write to Mrs Hennessey and explain, once it's safe to do so. But we can't go back. If they take Catherine they might kill her."

He spoke bluntly and his wife was convinced.

"You too, young Rosie," he said, "you're very welcome to come with us and be part of our family. Molly tells me you lost your memory and don't know who you belong to. Well, we'd like you to belong to us!"

Mrs Dalton nodded and Catherine grinned with delight.

Before Rosie could answer, Mr Dalton went on eagerly, "In three or four months I shall have enough saved for us all to go to America. What do you think of that?"

Catherine's eyes lit up. Mrs Dalton said, "That would be wonderful! There are no jobs for you in Dublin and we know no one in Manchester. If we go to America we can stay with my sister Mary and her family in New York. You might even make your fortune, Henry!"

Rosie briefly wondered what her life would be like if she set sail for the States in 1920. But she was not tempted. "I can't go with you," she said and Catherine was deflated.

"Why not, Rosie? We could have such times! And we could write to William – I'd still go to Australia – you could too. Think of the adventures!"

"I have to find my family and go back to them," Rosie said.

She was determined and Catherine knew she would not be swayed. Remembering how much she'd missed her own father, she said, "I hope you find them soon, Rosie. But promise me, once the Tans leave the tenement, you'll visit Mrs Hennessey. She'll find you somewhere safe to stay until your memory comes back."

Rosie nodded.

"Molly, we should leave now," Mr Dalton interrupted, "with as little fuss as possible."

"Give me a few minutes. My clothes are in the locker."

While Mrs Dalton made for the hospital washroom to dress herself and her husband waited in the corridor, Rosie took Catherine to one side. "You must write a note to Lilian," she said. "I know you intend to write, but something could go wrong, like with your father's letters. I'll make sure she gets it." The programme for the Carlton cinema was still in her pocket. "Write on the back of this," she said.

Borrowing a pencil from her father, Catherine filled the blank sheet on the back of the programme, folded it in two and handed it to Rosie.

They looked at each other. "How will I get in touch with you, Rosie? If you go home?"

Knowing they would never meet again, Rosie could not say so. She swallowed. "I'll keep in contact with Lilian," she said and Catherine brightened.

"That way she'll be able to send me your address and I can write. Oh Rosie, I'm glad I met you. You brought me such luck!"

Rosie did not see it. "How can you say that? If I hadn't turned up at the Gresham this morning, Brown wouldn't have told on us and you'd be able to go home. You wouldn't be emigrating to America."

"But America is an adventure! And, Rosie, since you came I've had food to eat and we had a wonderful party and Mother is better and Father came back for us. You brought me luck all right, and I'll never forget you."

By now Mrs Dalton was ready and Rosie traipsed down the stairs with them past the bustling nurses and doctors and crowds of waiting patients. No one paid any attention.

"I hear none of the trains are running," Mr Dalton said, "but they haven't stopped the trams yet. We'll have to take a cab from Dalkey."

At the Pillar terminus, Rosie shook hands with each of them. Catherine pressed her arm and said, "I'll write. Maybe you'll come with me to Australia to see William. Don't forget to let him know what's happened. Tell him I'll send a letter to the Gresham as soon as there's no risk of the Tans seeing it."

She stepped after her parents on to the tram and she and Rosie waved to each other until it curved away across O'Connell Bridge.

Chapter 18

IT WAS dark now. Most of Dublin's citizens were indoors. Trams rattled along from the terminus practically empty. Only the Crossleys broke the silence, their wheels always screeching for effect.

Rosie crept down the back lane behind the Gresham, ready to run at the first sight of a Tan. In the kitchens she found Hugh Callaghan. He looked tired and anxious.

"We're all safe," she said immediately. "William went straight to Inchicore after he got out of Croke Park." She told him then about Catherine. "Be sure to tell William she'll write to him. But it won't be for a while, in case the Tans intercept the letter."

"Why don't you tell him yourself when he comes back?"

Shaking her head, Rosie said, "I won't be here. Now that Catherine's gone, I'll go back to my family."

"Have you remembered where you live, then?"

She nodded, "Whitehall," and not wanting him to ask any questions she put out her hand. "Goodbye, Mr Callaghan."

"Goodbye, Rosie," he was somewhat bemused. "When you've settled back home, you must come and visit us, especially William!"

She swallowed. There was no chance of that, ever.

The city was silent as she made her way back to the tenement. It was seven o'clock. She prayed the Tans had left. Unless she got back into that room, she could not go home. It was there she had found her route to the past and there she would find her way back.

She was at the tenement steps when a figure emerged from the basement, frightening her half to death. Terrified, she took in the uniform. For a moment she was sure it was Brown. But when the man moved into the lamplight she recognised his partner.

"What are you going to do?" She could not control the tremor in her voice.

"I'm supposed to arrest you. Take you in for questioning." Seeing her anxiety, he added, "Don't worry. I'll tell them you never came back."

"But what about your friend? Isn't he with you?"

"If you mean Brown, he's no one's friend. He found out you and your pal were going to the match with the boy from the hotel, so he went along with the convoy. Promised to use his bayonet if he found any of you. He didn't, did he?"

Rosie shuddered and shook her head.

"Good. It's safe for you to go home now." He sighed. "I wish I could go home."

"Where are you from?"

"The East End of London. Best place in the world. It'd be nice to be there for Christmas with Mother and the rest. I've got a sister about your age. A right terror!"

He looked quite young, Rosie thought, even younger than Foley. It must be lonely living so far away, with scum like Brown, in a place where everyone hated you. Maybe he'd killed people. Maybe he'd felt he had to. She didn't want to know.

191

"I hope you get home for Christmas. And thank you for letting me go." She smiled.

The soldier nodded. He walked away from her and in a moment she heard him whistle. The tune was familiar. Then she remembered Foley's daft dance to the same air. 'It's a long way to Tipperary.' Foley's song had been brisk. The soldier's melody was slow and sad.

Rosie too longed for home.

She made her way silently up the stairs. Outside the Hennessey's door, she paused. It was mean, she thought, not to say goodbye, but she could not face Mrs H's kindly questions, or Lilian's probing eyes. She went on up.

Opening the door, she peered in, but there was no one in the room. The Tans had gone. Quickly, from their hiding place at the window she took the rucksack and camera and put the programme with Catherine's letter into the bag. Taking out the watch, she fastened it around her wrist and altered the date.

Looking out she tried to memorise the cobbled streets, the old-fashioned lamps, the woeful houses. *Maginni's Academy of Dance*, where a whole family had died. Pressing her face against the window, she closed her eyes. The longing for home became unbearable. She concentrated, focusing on Gran and Mom and Dad. Now she could hear voices.

"It's hardly a pleasure trip, Rosie."

"Your Gran needs you."

"Going away isn't always wonderful. Sometimes the best part is coming home."

Finally she remembered Uncle Jack's words, "You've found a route, Rosie. A route to the past and back again. All you need is determination."

Then, as quietly as she had come, she made her way

back down the stairs and outside, to the spot where she had found Catherine. From one of the windows a man looked out at her. Mr Dempsey? She waved her last farewell and closed her eyes.

Blackness. Silence. Distant voices. A rumble that became louder. Distinct footsteps. A light becoming brighter. Traffic.

Rosie blinked. Along the kerbside were parked cars. A couple of teenagers in jeans and Levi jackets passed. Across the road, instead of *Maginni's Dancing School*, was the *James Joyce Cultural Centre*. The houses were no longer destitute but magnificent. There was no foul odour. Now there was only the smell of traffic. A surge of joy swept through Rosie. "I'm back! I'm home. Oh, brilliant!"

She got the bus to Helena's house and her friend opened the door.

"Did everything go as planned?" Rosie was urgent.

"Well, I rang your house like you said and left the message and that was fine. But then my mother phoned your Gran."

Rosie nearly died. "Why? Why did she do that? She ruined everything."

"She rang your Gran because she wanted some information about bridge. I'd say she rang about five times."

"I'm done for," Rosie said, "totally *finito*. Now they're all going to want to know where I've been!"

Helena eyed her friend speculatively. "I'm a bit curious myself," she said; then, "You needn't worry. Your gran was never in. Mom calls her the gallivanting granny. She did wonder, though, why you were never in either."

193

"And what did you say?"

"I told her you were playing bridge too, that one of your gran's friends was sick and she made you play instead. I told her you were a champion bridge player 'cos your gran taught you when you were a baby. I said when you were in your pram you never got a rattle like other babies, just a deck of cards. Now Mom wants you to play with her group sometime."

Rosie was outraged. "But I hate bridge. Bridge is boring! I wouldn't have spent a week playing bridge with three old ladies!"

Her friend shrugged. "It was the best I could do. And you should be grateful I was so quick."

"I suppose so," Rosie muttered. "At least it's safe to go back now." And having promised Helena to tell her everything soon, she was at last on her way home.

"Did you have a nice time with your friend?" Gran was there when she arrived. Rosie nodded, hoping the old lady wouldn't probe.

Her grandmother was full of her own week. "Wonderful bridge," she sighed, "I improved my bidding no end."

"Terrific," Rosie said, and not wanting Gran to ask awkward questions, kept firm control of the subject. "What was your best game?"

Gran was off, describing two no trumps, north-south positions, singleton spades, and other alien moves in ecstatic tones.

Rosie yawned her head off. When at last she noticed, Gran was instantly apologetic. "I am rabbiting on, amn't I? Look, I'll get us a nice cup of tea and a slice of your favourite gurcake. I made some especially for you." Her granddaughter wondered where she'd found the time.

194

As soon as Gran left the room, Rosie hastily scanned Catherine's note for any mention of herself. There was none. She found the box of papers and slipped in the programme.

Half an hour later, when she'd devoured the last crumbs of gurcake, Rosie said, "Gran, remember what we were talking about last week – about when you were young and about your friend Catherine. Could I have a look at her letters again? They might be useful for my project."

"Of course," said Gran.

The box on her knee, she rifled through the papers once more. Rosie saw the sepia tint of the programme. Gran didn't notice it, but went on sifting.

"What's that?" Rosie leaned over and plucked at the edge of Catherine's message.

"What? I don't remember that . . ." she picked it out. "Oh look – it's an old cinema programme. I recall the picture. *A Daughter of the East*, featuring Miss Lily Jacobsen. She looks as if she has black eyes, doesn't she? I went to this with Catherine and that girl."

"What's the writing on the back?"

At last her grandmother looked at Catherine's note. As she read, Rosie saw her brows lift in astonishment. Then her grandmother sat quite still, staring into the past.

"What does it say, Gran?"

"It's a note from Catherine. How did I miss it all these years?"

"You never opened the programme, that's how."

Her grandmother nodded. "That must be it. I never paid any attention to it. She must have slipped it under the door and when I found it I just put it away. That's the only explanation. But I wish I'd seen it before, Rosie, I wouldn't have worried about her so much."

Rosie saw the old lady's eyes fill. Gently she said, "Read it to me, please." And slowly Gran read:

To Lilian Hennessey 21st November 1920

Lilian, I am at the hospital. Father has arrived and I have told him the Tans are at home watching out for me. He is taking me and Mother over to England immediately. We are not to go back to the room at all. So I cannot say goodbye properly.

But Father has great plans for us, so you needn't worry. In a few months time I will write to you, but not before, as Father says agents could read the letters and the police might want to interview anyone who was connected to what happened today.

I will miss you, and William too. Tell him that for me. Of course I will write to him as well to say all our plans for Australia are still the same. You and he were the best of friends to me.

Till we meet again.

With fondest love,

Catherine.

"Of course, we never did meet again," Gran murmured. "Oh, I hope she had a happy life."

"I wonder why she never wrote," Rosie said.

"Maybe she did. But we moved away from the tenement in January. Father was offered a position on a farm in Meath, with a cottage. There would have been a new family in our room. They mustn't have bothered to find out from the neighbours where we'd gone." She sighed, "A letter with childish handwriting. I bet they didn't think it was important. I didn't come back to Dublin till I was eighteen. No one I'd known was still living in the tenement."

The note had tugged at her memories and she was content to sit lost in the past, but Rosie was still curious.

"She was very fond of William. I wonder did she ever get to Australia with him?"

Gran looked up and her eyes were sombre. "In a way, I'm glad she left when she did. At least she never found out what happened to William."

Rosie's heart jolted and she felt a sharp pain.

"What about him?"

Gran stared into the bleak distance. "He was killed, Rosie. That day in Croke Park."

Devastated, Rosie managed, "You never told me. He can't have died. You saw the newspapers – "

"I was only looking for Catherine's name. William didn't escape. And anyway the papers didn't have all the details for a while. It was the following week before his name was published and the circumstances of his death."

"But Gran, he made it to the exit. You thought he was safe. You told me so."

"Yes, but I didn't finish his story. We were concentrating on Catherine, remember? Father saw William at the match and was certain he was safe because he was near the gate. But he must have changed his mind and tried to cross the pitch. Maybe the exit was too crowded. His body was found at the foot of the bank. He didn't escape, Rosie. He was bayoneted, and all his bright ambitions died with him."

Eyes blurred, Rosie remembered Catherine's words:

"Nothing will happen to us. We have so many plans for the future, me and William. I don't believe anything will go wrong. It wouldn't be fair."

She saw him again. A tall confident boy among the cheering crowds, he was smiling down at her from the stands, waving in the afternoon sunlight.

Chapter 19

BUT GRAN was wrong about William.

Dad and Mom arrived home on Monday night. Normally they would have been full of their trip, the hotel, Dad's meetings, the museums, the concerts. Normally they would have enquired how the week had been for Rosie and Gran. Now all they wanted to talk about was someone Dad had met at a conference.

"A fellow from Sydney, there to explore marketing possibilities for a chain of hotels in Europe," Dad told them. "A good sort. He was on his own and a bit lonely, so I asked him out to dinner on Saturday night with myself and Madge. You won't believe the rest of this – "

"His parents were from Dublin," Madge cut in. "Out of politeness we asked what part." She shook her head, as if still unable to believe the stranger's answer. "His mother lived in North Great Georges Street up to 1920. Her name was Catherine Dalton. Well, of course, that immediately rang a bell after all the stories you told me about your childhood, Mother."

"And his father worked in the Gresham hotel as a boy." Dad was eager to make his contribution again. "This chap said his mother was always talking about her childhood and particularly about one friend . . ." He paused for effect and was quite miffed when Madge cut in again, "You know who the friend was, Mother. You! Lilian Hennessey!"

By now Gran was clutching her throat, unable to speak. Rosie's mouth had dropped open.

"What . . . ?" Gran faltered, overcome.

"What was his father's name?" Rosie managed it for her."

"William Scott!" Mom and Dad spoke together, each determined to get in first with the news.

"But . . ." Gran tailed off again, unable to cope with the shock.

"But William was killed in Croke Park, on Bloody Sunday, the 21st of November 1920."

It was her mother's turn to be shocked. "She knows some history!" Mom's voice was faint. "Our Rosie actually knows some history!" Dad grinned and patted her hand.

"What about William?" Rosie asked through gritted teeth.

"His son – Robert – said his father was wounded in Croke Park," Dad told them. "Apparently he couldn't stay in the hospital though, because the Black-and-Tans were after him. Once he got the wound dressed, his uncle smuggled him on to a ship sailing to the Far East."

"Then what happened?" At last Gran was able to speak.

"We don't know. It was getting late and Robert said he wanted to go back to the hotel and ring his mother immediately to let her know he'd found her old friend. He was leaving early the next morning so we didn't see him again. But he took our address and I'm sure his mother will write – "

"You mean she's still alive!" Gran was overjoyed.

"And William?" Rosie asked, half afraid.

199

"Still going strong except for a touch of arthritis," Dad told her. He looked at her curiously. "I must say, Rosie, it's wonderful to see you taking such an interest in the old days!"

A week later the letter arrived.

Gran opened it with trembling fingers and Rosie, much to her parents' amused astonishment, sat close beside her at the table ready to read it too.

"Rosie, that's a private letter," Mom said.

"Not at all. Leave the child alone. Hasn't she the right, after all the interest she's taken!"

Mom and Dad were amazed. As far as they knew, Rosie had never looked at Gran's old photograph, and had barely suppressed groans when she'd talked about her childhood.

Rosie smiled gratefully at Gran and they perused the letter together.

> Scott's Grand Hotel
> Sydney Harbour,
> Sydney,
> 22 November '95

Dear Lilian,

I could not believe it when Robert phoned to say he'd met your daughter and her husband in Brussels. What amazing luck!

You know, William and I have been back to Dublin many times over the years and we've visited all the old haunts in the hope of finding some trace of you. I used to imagine you'd come walking around the corner of North Great Georges Street and all the years since childhood would disappear.

Often William and I had afternoon tea in the Gresham, thinking it was just possible you'd stroll in.

Never in a million years would I have guessed our children would meet before we did. And not in Dublin or Sydney, but in Brussels, where none of us has any ties. Isn't life extraordinary?

Well, Lilian, to give you some idea of what has happened to us:

In March 1921, I left Manchester for America with Mother and Father. A number of letters to you got no reply. When I realised you must have moved, I wrote at once to Mrs O'Brien for a forwarding address. The letter was returned unopened, with a stiff little note to say the addressee no longer lived in this residence which was now empty due to the dangerous condition of the building. The message was initialled, with no indication who'd sent it.

I knew then I'd have to wait a few years to make contact, but never thought it would take three-quarters of a century!

With William I had better luck, though not at first. I wrote to the Gresham and got a letter back almost immediately from Mr Callaghan to say William was dead, killed in Croke Park. Oddly enough, I didn't believe that. William couldn't have died, I thought, without my knowing. So I was not surprised to get another letter from Mr Callaghan in June '21, telling me he was on board a ship for the Far East, recovering from a bayonet wound. He enclosed the address of his next port of call and that is how I found William.

I'll never forget our meeting in Sydney Harbour when I was twenty.

He was so tall, Lilian. For some reason I'd been expecting the fourteen-year-old boy I'd last seen, not

201

the young man who was waiting for me on the quayside.
He must have been taken aback too, because neither of
us spoke for ages. I was getting desperate, trying to
think of the right thing to say. Then he smiled and he
looked fourteen again. And I gave him a dig in the arm
because I still couldn't speak and he said, "Well, I see
you haven't changed after all!"

And everything was fine from then on.

We did everything we set out to do, Lilian, except
come back to Ireland to live. We never realised how much
we'd grow to love this country and we've had such a
lucky life here.

In our younger days we travelled all over Australia.
We married six months after I came out here and had
four children. Robert is the eldest. Then there's Catherine,
(called after you) Hugh and Rosemary — Rosie for short,
after the girl who stayed with me the week before I left
Ireland. Do you remember her? We never found her again
either, though I have the feeling she might be still alive.

Our sons and daughters are married and we have ten
grandchildren. The business has flourished. Of course the
children run the hotels now. Sometimes when I walk
through the plush lobbies I think of where we came from.
But it's not the dismal poverty I remember, it's the
parties we had and the songs and especially the people.
They were *so* warm hearted.

William and I live in the Sydney hotel. We have a suite
of rooms and the staff are very respectful and the
children and grandchildren couldn't be nicer. But I
dream of the old days when I robbed Mrs O'Brien's snake
and we looted Findlater's. I remember the pawnshops
and the Guinness barges. Sometimes I even miss your
mother's fish-head stew!

Lilian, please write back immediately. I want to know

all about your life and we haven't too much time left. William sends his fond regards. He cannot write because of his arthritis, but otherwise he is in good health and as nice and kind as ever.

    Write soon.

    Your best friend,

    Catherine.

Gran and Rosie sat back.

"She's had a good life," Gran murmured, "and she's happy. Imagine one of her children having the same name as you, Rosie. Imagine if your father hadn't gone to Brussels . . ."

"We'd never have found out William was alive," Rosie said, "or what happened to them in Australia."

They sat side by side, thinking about the letter, while Rosie's parents waited impatiently to hear what was in it. After all, it was because of them it arrived at all!

I bet William and Catherine had wonderful adventures together in Australia, Rosie thought. I bet they were brave and daring. And I bet they had great fun.

There was only one way to find out. "Do you think I could write to Catherine, Gran?"

"Of course! What a good idea."

Rosie studiously avoided her parents' astonished eyes.

THE END

About the Author

Ann Carroll was born and educated in Dublin. She studied English and French at UCD, holds a Master's degree in Anglo-Irish Studies, and teaches English in Killinarden Community School, Tallaght. She is married with two children and lives in Dublin. *Rosie's Troubles* is her second book for Children's Poolbeg.